Midsummer

Suzanne Jenner

A Judy Sullivan Book

Walker and Company
New York

First published in the United States of America in 1985 by the Walker Publishing Company, Inc.

Published simultaneously in Canada by John Wiley & Sons Canada, Limited, Rexdale, Ontario.

Library of Congress Cataloging in Publication Data

Jenner, Suzanne.
  Midsummer.

  "A Judy Sullivan book."
  I. Title.
PS3560.E517M5 1985   813'.54   84-20977
ISBN 0-8027-0831-5

Printed in the United States of America

10 9 8 7 6 5 4 3 2 1

Chapter 1

THE PRIVATE JET dipped into an air pocket, and Carol's fingers clutched the arm rests as though her grip could halt the sickening descent. She drew a sharp breath and stared intently at the oak-paneled wall inside the airplane. The plane soon settled back onto an even path of substantial air, but still she held on.

"You are holding the plane up by the arm rests, *stakkars liten?*"

The Scandinavian lilt in the voice from across the wide aisle was pleasant, and there was a smile on the young man's face, but it was a patronizing smile, as though to a child. Still, the words were the first personal ones she had heard since beginning this sudden journey.

"I've ... never flown before," she confessed.

"Ah! Then this is an adventure for you. A maiden voyage!"

"Yes, I suppose it is."

"Then we must find something to make it less frightening. If you will loosen your grip of death, I will place a drink in one of your little hands, ya?" Without waiting for her reply, he rose and walked to the small but well-stocked bar which was built in the forward part of the cabin. "Perhaps something mild for a virginal event ..." He proceeded to examine the labels on the bottles, removing them one by one from their individual, padded compartments.

Carol unclenched her hands from the leather arms of

her chair and massaged them self-consciously in her lap "Rhys Christiansen," he had introduced himself as they boarded the plane. "Rhys, rhymes with kiss." He had obviously been drinking—just how much, Carol could not tell, but certainly enough to make him slightly unsteady on his feet. For a terrifying moment, she was afraid he was the pilot. She was soon reassured to see two neatly uniformed men with *Nordsjøolje* and "North Sea Petroleum" emblazoned on their lapels climb into the pilots' cabin and sit at the controls.

Carol didn't know if Rhys-rhymes-with-kiss was related to the Tor Christiansen she was to meet in Oslo, since the surname was as common in Norway as her Smythe was in England. Until he spoke just now, it hadn't mattered, for Carol was too involved with her first-flight fear to pay attention to the lean young man. He had been so distant since their take-off, sitting apart from her, gazing out his porthole at the disappearing eastern coast of England in silence.

They were about an hour into the flight, and Carol was finally able to unlock her head from her tensed shoulders and look around the interior of the plane. It was an airborne office, with soft leather chairs and low tables anchored inconspicuously in deep, dark red carpet. A fine teak writing table dominated the cabin, placed to view the conference area in which she and Rhys were seated. They were the only passengers in the cabin, which was three times the size of Mr. Ballinger's office and her secretarial cubicle, and far more lavishly furnished.

Rhys came toward her with a crystal wine glass filled with a pale, shimmering liquid. He said, "You will find this comforting to both palate and stomach." She took it from him with a bravado she did not feel and thanked him briefly. But he did not back away. He leaned down and pulled a lever on the side of her chair. "See this. Your chair unlocks to swivel, to have the full view if you wish it."

She found herself moving in the chair smoothly to face out her window at a vast empty sky and the cold North Sea below. She said through clenched teeth, "Very nice, thank you," and managed a tight smile. Rhys Christiansen was obviously very aware of and amused at her discomfort. She had enough problems without having this arrogant young man teasing her. It was very annoying, especially at 30,000 feet over nothing but sea water and unreliable air.

She looked directly into his blond, Nordic face and said, "I'm quite comfortable now, thank you. Don't trouble yourself." He was about to protest when some impulse made her add, "I'm sure you prefer to drink alone."

The condescending smile left his face. He flushed, and Carol noticed a half-moon scar standing out whitely on his forehead, near the hairline. He nodded curtly and went back to his chair, settled into it, and closed his eyes.

Her words had been an echo of her mother's strident voice saying "You never could hold your whiskey—I'm married to a bottle baby." The clear memory of her father's defeated face had made her promise herself she'd never make a weapon of her tongue, as her mother had . . . never to use words to hurt.

The plane dipped and her seat swiveled loosely on its pivot, throwing the memory from her mind. She returned her seat to a forward position and locked it. She didn't need any superfluous movement; the dip and rise of the plane was quite enough.

The wine was sweet and warm in her mouth. She rolled it around her tongue, and in spite of her nervousness, relished the smooth, heavy feel of it. She swallowed, took a deep breath, and considered her situation, now so dramatically different from what it had been at eight o'clock that morning. So much had happened so quickly.

The drive in her rattling old Morris from her small flat to the office had been grayer and damper than usual along the London streets. It had rained most of the night, and the fog, rare in June, still lay heavy and close on the damp streets. But she had noticed little on that normal, routine drive, the route she had driven every working day for three years. They had been three pleasantly regular years. On the drive to and from her job, only the degree of grayness varied—the cracks in the gray concrete widened and were patched with gray, the gray buildings were sunlit or shadowed but always gray, the lampposts' dark silhouettes were gray-black in the asphalt-gray streets.

She recalled looking forward to seeing Mr. Ballinger off on a trip to Norway for a field consultation. At last she would have a few days to organize the clutter in his office without his presence. The Chief Engineer of McKinzie Marine, Ltd., was scheduled to leave that afternoon. Mr. Ballinger was a pleasant man to work for, always vaguely embarrassed about asking Carol to do any work, even though she constantly assured him that she preferred to keep busy. Often she would have to insist that she type up the notes written haphazardly on scraps of paper or copy the figures scrawled on the slate board mounted on the wall of his office before he absent-mindedly erased them to start another computation.

After three years of working with him, Carol could generally comprehend the beginning, middle and end of various projects, though she had little idea what any individual figure meant. The designs for the mammoth platforms that held the giant offshore oil drilling rigs in the wild waters of the North Sea were a mystery to her. But with very few questions, she could decipher the scribblings and put the intricate drawings in order, then send them on to be drafted by the younger engineers. She was more than a competent secretary. Appreciated in a vague way by the amiable genius she worked under, she was considered indispensable by Mr. McKinzie, the president. He believed, with some evidence, that Ballinger's genius would be lost to the company, the United Kingdom, and

4

the oil-starved world if little Carol Smythe did not keep the figures, decipher the notes, and organize "our brilliant madman's scribbles!"

It was, all in all, a pleasant job, and Carol felt secure in the familiar structured atmosphere. After her escape from her unpleasant home, then the drudgery of secretarial training, McKinzie Marine seemed a haven. Her work was nearly always interesting, often challenging, and she enjoyed the satisfaction of doing it well. The highly technical nature of her job, and the work of the company itself, represented an abstract precision Carol found safe and comfortable.

This gray morning was no different from any other until she turned her car into the street in front of the office building, the monolith that housed McKinzie Marine. A shiny white ambulance seemed brilliant in the gray. An attendant shut the rear ambulance doors, hurried around to the front and got into the cab. The siren screamed as if in pain, and the vehicle roared away, tearing the mist violently from the street.

It was half an hour before she was able to understand what had happened. The office staff, arriving on the scene one by one, all had more questions than answers. After the night watchman, who had discovered the unconscious Mr. Ballinger, had explained that fact for the hundredth time, everyone was finally convinced that it had happened.

For a time, Carol and the others hovered about, speaking in hushed, anxious voices, morbidly excited by the break in the routine. At last each wandered regretfully to his or her desk and began the day's work.

Carol too went to her desk and stared at the immaculate surface. It was unmarred by a single stray scrap of paper or misplaced pencil, and the in-out box was neatly squared at one corner. She went into Mr. Ballinger's office and looked at the contrasting chaos of creativity. On his desk was the open briefcase they had packed together the previous afternoon—a dozen file folders bulging with scrawled figures, formulas and sketches. She glanced at the top page, and the sight of the quixotic mathematical shorthand of Ballinger brought a rush of sadness to her. She even felt tears in her eyes.

Mr. McKinzie boomed into the office at that moment, a short, grizzled Scotsman with little tufts of white hair standing straight out behind his ears. His face, normally ruddy, was flushed vermillion, and his usual soft Scottish burr rattled about the room as he addressed her.

"Finally got an answer from the hospital! It would be a stroke, not a bad one. He'll live to drive us mad another day!"

Carol began to voice her relief at knowing Mr. Ballinger would recover, but Mr. McKinzie rolled on.

"But it's today that's our worry, m'girl! Ballinger was to meet with Tor Christiansen in Oslo this afternoon with the preliminary plans. His company plane leaves at one o'clock, and Ballinger was to be on it!"

Carol began, "Then I suppose you must . . ."

"Can't, m'girl! Booked solid for the week with the board and the bank! And the Saudis are coming in tomorrow! Besides, I don't know a thing about the new float. You know that . . . I'm from the old days of the compass and protractor. Don't know a thing about these damn computers. M'head is full of credits and debits, mostly debits, and not much else!"

"Then will one of the other engineers . . . ?"

"Numbskulls, all of 'em! Overpaid robots!" He pointed at the briefcase. "Are these his notes?"

"Yes, we packed them yesterday."

"You know what's in here?"

"Well, yes, as much as anyone besides Mr. Ballinger . . ."

"You're wrong, m'girl! It's the future of McKinzie Marine that's in here! We can only hope Ballinger has kept Christiansen up on the concepts so he can understand these

6

notes when he reads them. And to make sure, you're going with these notes to Oslo! Heathrow, one o'clock, North Sea Petroleum hangar."

"But Mr. McKinzie, I don't have a passport, or a visa . . ."

"You don't need a visa, and you can get an emergency passport at the passport office. Take your certificate of birth, some pictures of your pretty self, and some worthy British subject who's known you for several years. I'll pull some strings so you won't have to queue up in the bloody line for too bloody long. How have you lived this long without a passport, m'girl?"

Before she could answer, he rushed on, "Here's a few pounds cash and the company credit card. Be a good girl and don't use it. Take the notes, go home and pack whatever you need. Stay there as long as Christiansen wants you. I'll call and tell him the situation."

He paused and looked at her. "For heaven's sake, it's not the end of the world, just a bit of a trip. Now get to it!"

McKinzie boomed out of the office still talking. Carol heard him shouting his way down the hall. "Deliver the goods. And if Christiansen can't decipher the notes, do it for him, the same as you do for the rest of us! Curse that Ballinger." A door slammed and there was silence

Things like this didn't happen! Not to her, she'd made sure of that. Stay in control, plan, organize—avoid the unexpected. But she had an assignment, and she had no choice but to see it through. She closed the briefcase and rushed out of the office. There wasn't enough time!

As she hurried through the lobby of McKinzie Marine, she passed the dusty old display case there, full of miscellaneous artifacts of the sea and the instruments her company used to delve into its depths and take its treasures. Suddenly her eyes were caught and held by an ancient wooden plaque, inscribed in Latin. She read the words "*A furore normanorum, libera nos, O Domine*—From the Norsemen's fury, deliver us, Oh Lord."

7

Carol quivered involuntarily. Was it an omen? She shrugged at her silliness. She did not over-dramatize anything. This trip to the land of the Norsemen was simply business, and she must get on with it.

She reflected on omens no more. She drove home, ran into the house and was, of course, unable to avoid her omnipresent landlady.

"'Ome at this 'our, dearie?"

"Yes, Mrs. Pickett. I'm flying to Norway."

"Norway? Now?"

"Yes, I'm in a hurry, so . . ."

"Well," sniffed Mrs. Pickett through her eternal cold, "la-dee-dah! Off to a foreign land! And you, who's never been to Brighton!"

Carol stopped cold, her key in the door. McKinzie's words echoed, ". . . some worthy British subject who's known you . . ."

"Mrs. Pickett, you've got to come with me to the passport office! I need to verify my existence!"

"To what your what, dearie?"

"Identify me! So I can get an emergency passport!"

"Oh, I don't know . . . I 'aven't been feelin' at all well . . ."

Carol took the money McKinzie had given her and waved it in front of Mrs. Pickett's runny nose.

"We'll take a taxi! And you can take one back, and stop for tea if you'd like, or the pub . . ."

"Well, I suppose I might, since you put it that way. Always like to help out when I can."

"I'll be packed in fifteen minutes!"

Carol went into her flat and closed the door against Mrs. Pickett's next violent fit of coughing. She packed one small grip, decided she hadn't time to clean out the fridge, put a few more pins in her hair and rushed out again.

Mrs. Pickett had donned a red hat for the excursion, and fortified herself with a supply of tissues. All during the taxi ride and the two-hour wait in the line at the emergency passport section, Carol listened to Mrs. Pickett's life story, punctuated by sneezes, coughs and sniffs. By the time the passport was secured and Mrs. Pickett dispatched by taxi Carol was a nervous wreck, *and probably contaminated*! she thought.

Somehow she managed to arrive at the private hangar of North Sea Petroleum by noon. She hoped to have some time to catch her breath. But Rhys had been waiting and as she was the only other passenger, he had ordered the pilot to take off immediately. She had been airborne before she'd known what was happening.

The sound of the engines seemed quieter now, and the wine had settled her nerves a bit. She dared a glance out the window and became fascinated with the clouds beneath her. The steadiness of the craft calmed her. She relaxed and decided that she was indeed having an adventure. She looked over at the blond young man who seemed to be in charge of her and the Ballinger notes. Rhys was tall and lean, the chiseled Nordic bones lying close under the fair skin of his long face, his thick, straight blond hair groomed perfectly, combed back from a high forehead. There was something about the mouth—a slackness, perhaps, and a paleness around his eyes that indicated his drinking was not just occasional.

Suddenly Rhys' eyes opened and he looked at her. Carol looked away in some confusion, partly because she had been caught staring and partly because the vivid blue of his eyes held her own gaze much longer than polite interest decreed. She fumbled aimlessly in her handbag.

"There is a rest room in the tail, if you wish to freshen up." The Nordic melody in Rhys' voice and the kindness behind his offer of this mundane piece of information added to Carol's fluster.

"Thank you. I would like to powder my nose."

She was caught by her seat belt in her effort to rise. He grinned at her and she was forced to smile back thinly. It seemed she would continue to embarrass herself in front of him. She unfastened the belt and got to her feet, tentatively testing her balance, and then strode to the tiny door at the rear of the plane with more poise than she felt.

She closed the door of the compartment and started at the image that confronted her in a full length mirror. Her gray linen work suit and the paler gray, tailored blouse were not only dull, they were now badly wrinkled. Her face was pale and tense—overall, a discouraging picture.

Carol powdered the few freckles which sprinkled her nose and jabbed some rebelling curly wisps of her thick auburn hair into the severe twist at the back of her neck. That would have normally completed her make-up, but the thought of the grinning young man with the lilting voice in the cabin outside made her dig into her bag for a seldom-used case of blush and apply some just under the fine bones of her cheeks. She stared at herself and frowned, then wiped the offending pink from her face with a tissue.

What am I doing? she thought. *I'm here for business purposes, not seduction!* Then she laughed at the thought of Carol Smythe seducing anyone. *When would I have had the chance to Practice? And on whom? The married accountants or engineers at the office? I'm not the type and I never will be. Back to business. I've an important job to do, and Mr. McKinzie trusts me to do it.*

She emerged from the room and smiled at Rhys, now airworthy and confident, her legs steady under her. Immediately the plane lurched and she stumbled into a chair, which swiveled out of her hands and threw her against the wall of the plane. Stunned for a moment, she felt strong hands grab and hold her.

"Not to worry, little *mus*. You are safe in the corporate arms of North Sea Petroleum, ya?" Rhys kept one strong arm around her as he led her to her seat. "The maiden must be a little more careful until the adventure becomes familiar. Then you will ride easy."

"Thank you, you're very kind." And this time she meant it. She sat down and fastened her seat belt quickly. "What does *mus* mean?"

"It is 'mouse' in English . . . little gray mouse, ya?"

Carol bridled a bit at the analogy, never having thought of herself as any kind of animal, and certainly not a mouse.

"Ya, a little English *mus*." Rhys was pleased with the image. Carol quite forgot herself and spat out, "You might find that English mice have very sharp teeth!"

Rhys laughed, the laugh making his sneering smile disappear into a boyish handsomeness. "And also spirit, ya?" He reached over and touched her arm, and the warmth of his hand went through the cloth of her linen suit. "We have time for a little *snitter*, and some more wine. It makes the time go."

"I don't need to be waited on," Carol said abruptly, disturbed by his manner as well as his touch.

"I think you do. Forgive my lack of attention. I haven't been feeling very well today. You were right before . . . too much drink these past days in London, too much even for me."

The delicate little sandwiches he placed on a table near her were works of art—swirls of fish and flowers of vegetables arranged on tiny pieces of white bread. Rhys poured her more wine and a glass for himself, then sat next to her.

"You will find I am good company when I am sober, and even better when I am drunk. It is only when I have the hangover I am not interesting."

"You have a very good opinion of yourself."

"Ya, I do."

The striking blue of his eyes seemed to appraise her, commenting on her grayness, her mousiness, her . . . She looked away from the eyes and down to the tray of sandwiches. Why should she care what he thought? She picked up a small, beautiful sandwich.

"It looks too good to eat."

"They are works of art, but they are to devour, please."

Rhys began to describe the different kinds of fish on each of the sandwiches. Carol ate and nodded while she pondered the sensation she had felt when his strong arm held her, almost carried her to her seat when she stumbled. She wished it had not happened, and she found it difficult to meet the blue eyes that paid so much attention to her now, however critical that attention was. She must get hold of herself. It was probably just the new environment, the strangeness of the situation. She wished herself back in her little rattling Morris on the safe, gray London streets. But she wasn't there; she was here—high over the sea in the company of a sophisticated and, in spite of himself, charming young man.

"You live alone in London?" His question was polite.

"Yes. My mother died several years ago, my father when I was a child. They were the only family I had, no brothers or sisters. I prefer to live alone."

"I too. But I do not have the advantage of no family. My mother is very much alive, in Bergen, and my little sister Lisle, also."

"Tor Christiansen is your father then, or uncle?"

Rhys turned his eyes from her and stared out the porthole opposite. His voice turned hard. "No, my brother."

"He's the one I am to meet with the papers."

"Of course. Tor is the one to meet for all important matters. I am only his errand boy."

"I am sorry you think of me as an errand."

The hardness left his voice if not his eyes. "But a very pleasant one, my little *mus*. And I'm sure it will become more so." His eyes traveled down her body, and even encased in her severe suit, Carol felt the penetrating blue

12

gaze on her skin. "Perhaps you will stay in Oslo for a time? There is much to see, to do. We will go on a tour, and to dinner. We have fine discos also." The blue eyes twinkled just a little. "I will keep you from falling down, once I get you unbuckled from your seat, I promise."

There didn't seem to be an ounce of reserve in the man, and Carol's own reserve seemed to be under attack.

"I am to return to London as soon as possible, but perhaps I will see at least . . . a fjord."

He laughed, "It will be difficult to avoid seeing a fjord."

"Is there any danger of falling into one?"

The laugh continued, genuine and not unkind. "I promise you that you will not fall into a fjord! I myself will hold you tight on the mountain top!"

Carol smiled at his delight but tried to keep her mission in mind. "I won't have time for mountain climbing. I have business with your brother and . . ."

"We must hope that will not take a long time. My brother is not amusing. All business . . . very boring. And that is when he is in a good mood."

"And when he isn't . . . ?"

"I would rather be in a *storm i fjellet,* a mountain storm. But that is better than the quiet anger, the kind that seethes under his ice and snow.

"He can't be that bad."

"You will see, little *mus.* But let us have no more talk of him. You will have more wine, ya?"

The intercom broke into her refusal with notice of their imminent arrival at Fornebu airport in Oslo. Carol put her glass down hurriedly and checked her seat belt. There was a sudden roaring shift of engines beneath them and the plane began a sharp, turning descent. Carol swallowed to clear her ears and forced her gaze out of the porthole. The sight made her gasp.

Coming up below them with terrifying speed was a panorama of jagged mountains and blue water, striking

13

cliffs covered with green and sheering off into rocks that slivered into the fjord like ragged knives. The scene was untamed, frightening, seen before only in two-dimensional glossy photographs in the windows of tourist offices. The speed of the craft and the scene below her held Carol immobile.

Soon the city appeared, on the bay of what she would learn was the Oslofjorden. The expanse of lush green accented with red and white soon separated into parks and rooftops, trees and streets. Her hungry eyes begged for more, but the plane rushed her down and onto solid earth before she could begin to feast on it. She hardly felt the wheels touch down. She looked over at Rhys, who was nonchalantly sipping a glass of whiskey, smiling at her evident excitement.

"We have arrived, all in one piece, ya?"

"Ya . . . I mean, yes. I was very nervous."

"But you like it anyway, the flying?"

"I think so, yes. And the countryside, the city . . . it's all so beautiful!"

"You must see it all up close. You will deliver your papers to the office. Then we will go to dinner."

"I wish we could see some of the city first. If we have dinner first, it will be too dark."

His laugh interrupted her protest. "It is midsummer, little *mus*! The sun will be with us most of the night. We have much time to see everything."

The plane rolled to a stop beside a hangar, the exterior steel and glass, chrome letters spelling out "North Sea Petroleum" in both English and Norwegian. The engines were shut off and the hatch was opened immediately. Carol managed to remember to unfasten her seat belt before trying to get up, gathered her briefcase and handbag, and walked to the exit. Rhys gulped down his whiskey and followed her. He took her suitcase and handed it to the uniformed attendant at the bottom of the ladder.

It was the feel of the air that struck her first—clear and cool and fresh. She almost held out her hand to touch it, and simply breathed it in with a kind of wonder. "It smells so clean!" she said.

"London mouse is not used to fresh air. All I smell is fuel. Come into the office. I will arrange things with customs, and get a car. Give me your passport."

Solid ground felt good beneath her feet. They hurried into a spacious office inside the hangar and Rhys spoke to a uniformed man seated at a desk. The office shone; there was no better word to describe it. Stark white walls glistened, enameled hard and bright. Vivid blue streaks of iridescent brightness swirled across the walls and ceiling and continued the pattern on the glass-like floor. It all seemed perfect.

Carol hated it. It was frigid, impersonal, designed to stun and then dismiss the human beings who passed through. Carol felt physically cold in the room.

"You are Miss Smythe?"

Carol turned to look up into eyes that matched the blue swirls of the walls. They belonged to a tall, blond woman who might have been carved in ice. Perfect. Perfect skin—pale and clear and translucent. Perfect body—tall and correct and graceful. Perfect dress—light blue and soft, some wonderfully clinging fabric folding a gentle collar around the long, thin neck, then wrapping around down to a tiny waist and flowing into a full skirt. Carol had never seen a dress like it. *I don't believe it has any seams!* she thought irrelevantly. She managed to control the rapid series of impressions enough to identify herself.

"Yes, I'm Carol Smythe."

"I am Solveig Folkdahl. Mr. Christiansen asked me to meet you, since I had to be here on other business anyway. I am to take you to the company apartment."

"How nice. But Rhys is arranging for a car."

"Then Rhys will have to un-arrange it." Solveig Folkdahl

smiled with white, perfect teeth. She turned from Carol, dismissing her for the moment, and walked across the shining floor toward Rhys.

When Rhys saw Solveig, his jaw tightened visibly. Carol did not understand what they said to each other, but the exchange seemed unpleasant. *He doesn't like her,* Carol thought, and this pleased her. She told herself she was being very foolish, picked up her bag and briefcase and tried to be patient.

It was hard. She wanted to leave this carved ice palace and go out into that fine air, to look at the red-roofed houses and green trees and brilliant water.

Finally Solveig turned and came back to her. Rhys followed behind, his face expressing something between a boyish pout and masculine distaste.

"Come, Miss Smythe. Rhys, take her cases."

Rhys obeyed, but his eyes burned coldly.

The ride in Solveig's car, a deep maroon Jaguar sedan, was tense because Solveig was a less than perfect driver, paying little attention to the road in front of her. At every intersection, Rhys made small sounds of disapproval, fear or direction.

"No, don't ... watch out for the ... get in the left ..."

But Solveig ignored him and proceeded with careful diction to point out the Oslo Cathedral, dating from 1699, and the University, famous for its murals by Edvard Munch. Shops and restaurants were described down to the price range and menu.

Finally, unable to ignore Rhys' strangled cries, Solveig said, "I don't know why everyone is so critical of my driving. I've never had an accident."

"That's because all of Oslo gets out of your way!"

Solveig laughed. "Oh, Rhys, that is foolish!" Then she turned to face him in the back seat as the car wove from one lane to another. "Is that true? Am I a menace?"

"A monster menace!"

Solveig laughed and seemed pleased at her reputation.

At last the Jaguar slowed in front of a tall chrome and glass office building with the North Sea Petroleum logo above the wide, impressive entrance. Solveig steered into a parking garage under the building, was waved in at the entry by another blue-uniformed guard, and parked in a space marked "Folkdahl." They all got out and walked directly to a small elevator, which Solveig opened with a key.

Even the elevator was elegant. The walls were beige leather trimmed in metallic blue. Solveig pushed a tiny button and immediately a feminine voice queried them in Norwegian. Solveig answered and the elevator began to ascend soundlessly.

Apparently the "company apartment" was the penthouse of the office building. Carol stared at the elevator doors and felt the walls close and cold around her. She shivered and tried to rid herself of the distinct feeling that she was locked in a padded cell. There had been too many feelings, strong feelings, that day. She simply wasn't used to them. Finally the cell came to a velvet halt and the doors opened.

Chapter Two

IT'S EITHER AN art gallery or an exclusive salon, Carol thought. *Surely nobody lives here.* Deep gray carpeting swept up to charcoal walls lit softly by indirect lamps. An abstract tapestry hung on the opposite wall, its vibrant colors slashing the neutral background. The only furniture in the windowless space was a low steel and glass table holding a crystal vase of perfectly arranged yellow roses.

Solveig moved efficiently out of the elevator and across the space to large double doors. She put her hand on the pewter latch and went in. "I will tell Mr. Christiansen you are here."

Rhys followed, his shoulders tensed in anger, the white scar evident on his forehead. He stopped in the entry and stood facing away from her. Carol thought, *She treats him like a little brother, or an office boy.* But when he turned to her, he was grinning.

"Welcome to the Hall of the Mountain King! All trolls will assemble immediately in the dungeon!"

Carol laughed aloud. She felt affection for Rhys Christiansen at that moment; not just sympathy for the treatment he had received, but for the way he managed to clown just when matters might have become ugly.

Rhys rolled his eyes and snarled, twisting his face into a gargoyle glare. "She is a dragon, that one!" Then he grinned and the face changed back into the smooth, handsome one as Carol muffled her laughter with her hand. He waved to her to follow as he said, "Come, we both need a drink! This is what Tor Christiansen calls 'home.' His least favorite troll welcomes you to it!"

Carol followed him, encouraged by his ease in the stark surroundings. She walked through the doors and into an enormous room filled with light. She looked past Rhys, standing there grinning at her, waiting for her reaction to the vastness before her. All the walls were made entirely of glass, through which the sun blazed. And above her were large skylights opening the sky to her view. She was drawn to the wall of windows, and as she edged nearer, an involuntary gasp escaped her lips. She felt as if she were standing on a precipice overlooking the city.

"See, little *mus,* the city of Oslo is at your feet!"

Carol found her voice. "How beautiful! It's a city of green! There are so many trees, parks. And the river ..."

"Fjord," Rhys corrected her. "The Oslofjorden. Even I never tire of looking at it."

He came close, gazing outward with her. "And to see it from here, so high, it gives one the feeling of power."

"Not for me. It makes me feel humble, more a *mus* than ever."

Rhys looked at her and smiled. He took her arm. "Come and sit. I will get us something to drink." He indicated a seating area in the lobby-like living room and then strode out of the room through an archway, shouting, "Inga! Love of my life! Your wandering prince is here! Some sherry! And *Jarlsburgost*! Quickly, or I perish!" Robust feminine laughter greeted him from a distant room as he disappeared.

Carol looked around the living room. It was sparsely, but expensively furnished. At one end stood a huge black leather sling chair with an acre of ottoman before it and an oval glass and chrome table. The objects on the table were so perfectly arranged, Carol would never have dreamed of touching any one of them. She was sure the heavy, black ash tray had never felt a cigarette ash, nor had the black candles in the crystal candlesticks ever been lit. Another vase of yellow roses exactly like those in the foyer stood centered perfectly, and Carol noticed that they were silk, not real. Built into one curved wall was a gray suede sofa that undulated invitingly. *It could seat twelve,* thought Carol as she sank into it.

Where was the clutter of everyday living? Where were the personal things that ordinary people collect and cherish? Tor Christiansen must be a robot, efficient and clinical. She remembered Mr. McKinzie saying, "Tor Christiansen not only owns the blasted company, he understands it!" There had been a note of grudging admiration in the statement, which had followed McKinzie's reading of a paper on hydrodynamics that Christiansen had presented at a conference on offshore drilling.

The infant business had few experts, and Tor Christiansen was one of those few. There had been a terrible disaster several years ago on one of the rigs. Many men had been lost. Vibratory phenomena and fluid mechanics problems combined with a welding deficiency were still being debated as causes. The plans she carried in the briefcase dealt with those matters. She recalled Mr. Ballinger saying softly, "These will not bring the men back from the bottom of the sea, but there must never be another such accident." Such a display of emotion was rare for him. He had then shrugged it off and gone back to mumbling about probabilities and materials physics, slashing his figures on the slate board with renewed vigor. However much the man fell into the stereotypical mold of the absent-minded professor, he was a gentle, caring human being.

Rhys shattered her thoughts as he entered with a trumpeting tenor, Wagnerian in melody and pretension. He carried a large silver tray laden with food and wine. He nonchalantly destroyed the symmetry on the glass table, shoving silk flowers and candlesticks aside to make room for the tray. He poured two glasses of wine and handed her one of them.

"Now," he said, moving close to her on the expanse of curving suede, "we must make elaborate plans to turn Oslo upside down."

Carol leaned forward to cut a piece of cheese and put breathing distance between them. "I can't make any plans at all. My purpose in being here is strictly business, and ..."

"Then we must change your purpose in being here, and then your purpose in life!"

"My purpose in life?"

"Yes. What is it?"

"I haven't the faintest idea!"

He smiled and closed the gap between them on the couch.

At that moment Solveig entered from another set of gray doors. She smiled coldly at them. "Tor will see you in a moment, Miss Smythe, if you can tear yourself away."

Rhys sprawled his length over the couch, deliberately putting his feet on the spotless suede. He lifted his glass to her. "Solveig is responsible for this cozy decor. She has the most prestigious decorating firm in Oslo."

"In Scandinavia," said Solveig, saving Carol from having to say something complimentary. "It is a company apartment, not a difficult assignment, as I am thoroughly familiar with Tor's personality and North Sea Petroleum's needs." She reached over the table to adjust the vase of roses, frowning at the tray of food and wine. It was clear that Miss Folkdahl had a proprietary interest in this place, perhaps even a territorial one.

"Tor," Solveig said, "is a man who wants his space efficient and organized. He dislikes clutter and cuteness."

Rhys popped a cracker into his mouth and said as he chewed it, "I, on the other hand, adore clutter and cuteness. What is your deepest feeling about this grave problem, Carol?"

Carol did not want to be a tennis ball between them in what must be a long-standing match. "I have no deep feelings on the matter. But don't let me stop the discussion. You both seem to be enjoying yourselves so much." Carol stood up and moved out of the range of fire, thinking that the wine must have loosened her tongue. She started toward the windows but was halted by a deep baritone, a new voice, from the gray doorway.

"Miss Smythe? Please come."

Carol turned and looked across the room at a tall, blond man whose shoulders seemed to fill the frame of the wide door. The dark, pinstripe business suit was perfectly tailored to the muscular body, the tie neatly, perfectly tied. But her glance was immediately riveted to the broad, strong face and the vivid blue eyes that held her own.

"I am Tor Christiansen. You have the papers?"

Cobalt blue, the blue of the fjord . . . Carol managed a nod and went to pick up her briefcase. "Yes, Mr. Christiansen, right here."

"Good. Please come into my office."

Solveig rose and walked quickly to Tor's side, placing her hand possessively on his arm. "Don't be long, Tor. Remember we have dinner reservations at Frognersaeteren." She turned and smiled brightly at Carol. "It's a wonderful place."

Christiansen didn't seem to notice the possessive hand on his arm. He said, "That is for later," and motioned Carol into his office. She moved past the powerful body that towered over her, then heard him direct his voice into the living room. "I'm sure we can depend on you and Rhys to see that our evening will please us all . . . if you two can, as Miss Smythe observed, stop enjoying yourselves long enough to plan it." Carol heard no humor in the remark.

He followed her into his office and closed the door. The

room was large, but it was filled by the man. She felt his size and strength as he gestured to a chair for her and sat in his own behind the massive desk. "Strong" was the word for him. Everything about him was strong — his broad shoulders, his carriage, his aura of command. He seemed to be confined in the room even though the severity of his attire was a perfect match to the stark, spare furnishing of it. Carol's office in London was populated with oil men, but they were the figurers, the conceptualizers, the accountants—pale men. This man could have picked most of them up in one hand and tossed them aside.

The telephone rang. He excused himself formally and answered it with a terse "Christiansen." But his whole manner changed as he listened to the voice on the other end of the line. The furrowed brow smoothed and the eyes seemed to soften. His voice spoke gently in his musical language, the vowels long and singing, the effect lyrical.

Carol welcomed the chance to study this man who had been described as an iceberg, even as a troll. The picture Rhys had given her was impossible to reconcile with what she saw before her. He was incredibly handsome—better looking than Rhys—the bones of the face strong and even, the skin smooth and tan under the thick, blond hair. The strength of his body was also in his face. There was the suggestion of easy, athletic grace; he looked as though he anticipated movement, his whole body alert and ready. And the voice—this was not a voice of ice. It was low and gentle, even soothing. She watched as his free hand played absently with a silver pen, the large fingers delicate, almost fondling. And something warmly tentative stirred inside Carol Smythe's gray, controlled self. She forced her eyes away from his hand and down to her own, which were moist in her lap.

She heard the telephone receiver placed in its cradle and looked up at him.

"Forgive me," he said, "but my mother must be answered with patience, especially when she is so patient with me." He almost smiled, then brought his features into stern focus as he addressed her and the matter at hand. "Now tell me what this is all about."

As quickly as she could, Carol recounted the events of the morning, including the imminent arrival of the Saudis. She was grateful the tremor in her body was not apparent in her voice. Ending her story, she said, "Mr. McKinzie felt that you should have this information today as promised. I'm familiar with the way Mr. Ballinger drafts his notes and was elected to deliver them to you."

Christiansen threw the pen into a drawer and slammed it shut. "Saudis? Appointments? McKinzie sends me a *secretary*? Are you telling me that Ballinger works entirely alone? He has no engineers under him?"

His loud angry questions startled Carol. No one in her office burst out like this. It so startled her that she responded without thinking. "McKinzie Marine is superbly staffed, as I am sure you know. We felt that putting these plans into your hands was a priority. Mr. Ballinger's illness is hardly the fault of the company."

"I see," he said coldly. "So now McKinzie feels he has fulfilled his responsibility. That's not the way I see it. I need to work through these plans with the designer. My entire week has been cleared for the process. The problems to be solved are urgent."

"Anything I can do . . ."

"Are you prepared to present the new studies on degradation of materials and metal fatigue? Has McKinzie sent me an expert in fluid mechanics?"

Carol stood up and moved the briefcase to the middle of his desk in a defiant presentation.

"No, Mr. Christiansen, I am not an expert in fluid mechanics. I *am* an expert in Mr. Ballinger's method of work. For three years I have deciphered his notes. I am at your service for translating anything that is unclear to you.

If that is not enough, I will make arrangements for a return flight to London."

She crossed her arms and stood straight, hoping that she looked decisive, competent. He stared at her, the blue eyes turning steely, their brightness clouding. She did not feel either decisive or competent.

"No flight," he said finally. "If you work for McKinzie, you work for me. You will stay until I have examined the notes. Sit down."

Carol felt a childish impulse to remain standing, to defy at least that order, but she sat down. She would have to stay as long as she was needed. She would have to do her job. But the idea of being locked up with this disturbing man frightened her. She would try to finish the work as quickly as possible and escape.

"I'm ready to begin immediately. I assume we will work through the weekend?"

"No, I have other plans."

"Then why was Mr. Ballinger coming here today?"

It was clear that Tor Christiansen was not used to being questioned. He said, "Ballinger was to have worked with several of my assistants, then with me beginning Monday. There is now no point in the weekend consultations."

Suddenly the clouds disappeared from his eyes. He leaned back in his chair and looked at her, the blue eyes appraising. She was terribly conscious of the travel wrinkles in her skirt, and she supposed her hair was a mess. She resisted the impulse to check for escaping wisps from the twist at the nape of her neck. She should have asked to freshen up before meeting those eyes.

She pulled an appointment book from her handbag and flipped to the current date. "What is the schedule you wish me to follow?" To her amazement, her voice was steady.

"Assuming I can make some sense of the files by myself this weekend, we will meet promptly at nine o'clock Monday morning, in Bergen."

"Bergen?"

"It is a west coast city. I prefer to work out of Bergen for a number of reasons. It is closer to our drilling office in Stavanger and has complete computer hookup to the rigs. Call my secretary and arrange to fly there Sunday night. Is that clear?"

Carol swallowed her anxiety at the thought of another flight after barely getting her land legs, but she made the necessary notes, writing more slowly than she needed to. When she looked up, the eyes were still staring at her. And from one broad shoulder, a second pair of eyes had taken up the appraisal.

"There is a cat on your shoulder," she said without thinking. She was not able to keep the amusement from her voice as she viewed the incongruous picture. A great ball of calico fur and long tail swishing around his neck simply did not fit. Tor's broad hand reached up and stroked one of the cat's ears.

"This is Hoppetussa. Her name means 'little thing that can't stay still.' She thinks she is the boss."

The hand and voice were gentle. All the defenses she had raised disappeared as the cat licked Tor Christiansen's ear. Denying the feeling and her confusion, she said, "I will make the arrangements and be in Bergen by nine o'clock Monday. Will that be all?"

"Yes, Miss Smythe, that will be all. When you speak to Mr. McKinzie, communicate my dissatisfaction as to how this matter has been handled." He had clearly dismissed her as he picked up a sheaf of papers and began to read. The cat still perched on his shoulder. Carol could hear the purr across the desk.

She got up and went out of the office without another word, closing the door behind her. She felt insulted and embarrassed, and yet strangely exhilarated. She was somehow challenged, not only to do what was required of her, but to prove Tor Christiansen's assumptions wrong— about McKinzie Marine and about herself. But whatever proving she might do, it couldn't begin until Monday morning.

She was free. The weekend stretched before her. An opportunity—one she had never had—an expense account, unexplored territory, free time. The confrontation with Christiansen would not spoil the days ahead of her. Until Monday, she would put him out of her mind. She would find a cozy hotel, have a hot bath and quiet dinner, and snuggle down with some tourist guide books to plot the gift of time.

Carol walked into the living room to find Rhys alone on the couch. He said, "I see you have survived. Good! Now we can get on with more important matters. We planned to wine and dine your Mr. Ballinger, and you have fallen heir to the plans. You have a dinner dress?"

Rhys obviously didn't realize that his brother had made very clear that Carol was a very poor substitute for Mr. Ballinger, and a number of plans had changed. She said, "Thanks, Rhys, but there is no need to entertain me. I have my schedule and will not intrude on you any more."

Rhys took her arm and almost pulled her down to the couch, but it was a friendly, teasing pull. "Intrude? What means this 'intrude'? You are our guest. We will have dinner at the Frognersaeteren in two hours!" He squinted his eyes and pursed his lips, and spoke in a high falsetto. "We have the honor of Solveig Folkdahl's attendance!" Then he pulled himself to his full height and rolled the next sounds deeply in his throat. "And of course, Tor Christiansen, Head Troll, will be our host!"

Carol laughed. He was a charming clown, and it was good to laugh after the tension in the office.

Suddenly she felt a weight in her lap, and eyes as green as her own stared up at her. The cat had decided to get acquainted. Carol scratched the ears as Tor had done, and the cat purred.

"See, Hoppetussa insists you come with us! And Hop-

27

petussa is the boss! Tomorrow we will see the city, just you and I. And we will go dancing all the night long. I am most available."

"But I must find a hotel ..."

"No, you will stay here! It is all arranged. This is the company apartment. It is arranged to accommodate guests."

Just like that! Carol was annoyed that everything was so arranged without her having anything to say about it. The days of freedom to do as she wished were to be forgotten—not that she objected to Rhys' company. And, she reasoned, any personal plans had better be forgotten. She could not be anything but cooperative and accommodating to her hosts for the sake of McKinzie Marine. She would have dinner with them, smile, try to prove herself worthy of her company by being worthy of theirs.

She addressed the cat, "Well, Hoppetussa, if you say so ..."

"Good!" Rhys covered her hand on the purring animal with his own, a friendly gesture that intimated more. "The dinner will be good but not long, and afterward we can go dancing ... no need to wait until tomorrow ... and then ..."

"And your brother, will he go dancing too?"

Rhys laughed. "Tor? No, Tor does not dance. Tor does not do anything that is not essential, that is not productive, that is not planned." He summed up his brother with "Tor does not play."

The voice from the other side of the room was calm but with an edge to it. "I have no need to play, when I have a little brother to do it for me." His words were to Rhys, but he was staring at Carol. Now what had she done?

The cat leaped out of Carol's lap and ran to Tor, who bent and gathered her up in his arms. "And the little brother plays very well. I'm sure you will enjoy him, Miss Smythe. And now, Rhys, have you introduced her to Inga? That must be done."

Either Rhys missed the condescending tone in Tor's voice or chose to ignore it, for he leapt up to obey cheerfully. "Inga! Of course. I'll get her."

Rhys loped out of the room, with the easy grace of an athlete. But Carol was sure his only athletic endeavors were on the dance floor. She looked at Tor, who watched his younger brother exit. He said, "Rhys used to ski the downhill."

Carol was taken aback. It was as though Tor Christiansen had read her thoughts. But of course, he was merely thinking the same thing as Rhys moved, a coincidence.

Carol questioned him, "And you? You ski too of course?"

Tor turned to her angrily. "I do not have time!" He took a steadying breath and spoke formally. "You have not been given time to freshen up. Please excuse our inattention. Inga will take care of you. I will see you as we go to dinner."

He turned and left the room. Her question about his skiing seemed ordinary enough to her, no reason that it should upset him. Perhaps assuming that all Norwegians skied was a foreigner's error and impolite. But she decided she would probably never have an ordinary conversation with the man.

"This is Inga!" Rhys' voice brought her back to the present. Standing next to him was a woman in her sixties. She wore her long, still-blond hair braided in great circles on top of her head. A large white apron covered her ample frame and her smiling face was open and kind. Inga held out both her big hands and clasped Carol's. In heavily accented English she said, "So! You come all the way from London, ya? Is your first time in *Norge*? Is beautiful country, ya? Come. Fresh coffee in my kitchen. Here we live from one cup of coffee to the next."

Suddenly a steaming cup of coffee sounded heavenly to Carol. Sharing that coffee in a kitchen with this cozy woman was what she wanted more than anything in the world. Her face must have reflected her feelings because Inga led her away by the hand without another word.

Rhys called after them, "I can't compete with Inga's coffee. I'll see you in two hours!"

The kitchen had put up a brave struggle to be sleek and ultra-modern like the rest of the apartment. But it had Inga to reckon with, and Inga had won. There were plants blooming on every window sill, brightly painted wooden plates hung on the walls, and gleaming copper kettles shining from a ceiling rack. There was a large, round wooden table and sturdy chairs with flowered cushions. In the center of the table a collection of carved wooden candlesticks held lit candles. The smells were wonderful—brewing coffee and something warmly cinnamon. The cat, who seemed to be everywhere, was curled on one of the chairs.

"You are surprised at my kitchen, ya?" said Inga as she poured cream into a crockery pitcher. "When I come here I ask where will I sit, where is a table? They tell me there is 'banquette.' And I say 'No, there is no banquette in Inga's kitchen.' So Tor tells them, in this kitchen must go whatever Inga says." Her low warm laugh filled the room as she piled a plate full of thick cinnamon cookies. "Eat. *Tekake* and *vørterkake,* ya? Oh, be careful of hot coffee. Pull in air as you sip."

Carol lifted the steaming mug to her mouth and dutifully pulled in air with the liquid. "It works!" she said after she swallowed the first delicious gulp.

"Ya," said Inga, "it works. Tell me all about England. Is very bad you have no fjords."

Carol found herself talking about her flat, the office, her few friends—how her work had taken over, filled up her life.

"I'm really very happy with the way things are." As she said them, the words sounded hollow and meaningless. She thought, *I'm lying to myself.*

30

Inga encouraged her with a chorus of "Ya's" and Carol opened herself to this warm stranger. She didn't give a thought to the time until Inga reminded her about dinner.

Carol put down her cup with a little moan. "Everything in my luggage will be wrinkled, and I'm all gritty from travel. Rhys said something about a dinner dress. I have something that I guess will do . . . I had to pack so quickly." The one dress in her wardrobe that "did" for a dinner dress was a pale green challis sheath, which was out-of-date. Being "in style" had never mattered much to Carol, and she wondered why it seemed to now.

"You are pretty girl. You wear dress; dress doesn't wear you." Inga was roused to action. "Hot bath first! I press dress, have ready. You want me start *badstu*?"

"No, thank you . . . just the bath will be fine." Carol didn't know what a *badstu* was, but she didn't feel she could try any more new things on this hectic day.

Inga ushered her into the guest room. It had the same gray walls and carpet as the rest of the apartment. One wall was floor-to-ceiling mirrors, reflecting a huge platform bed that seemed to float in space. The covering on the bed was a deep rosy beige velour, and it was flanked by pale birch tables. The wall of windows was partially concealed with vertical blinds that gave the room privacy from the city below. "It's a handsome room," said Carol, "but I'm happy to know your kitchen is right down the hall."

"And you come there any time!" said Inga and hurried her into the bathroom. "You be easy. I unpack for you."

As Carol soaked in the steaming tub, the tension slowly left her body. The events of the day, from her arrival at the London office until this lovely, warm moment, went through her mind like static at first, then mellowed and arranged themselves in calm order. The activities and emotions had piled up so suddenly, so vividly, she had almost been overwhelmed by it all. But now she was re-

31

laxed and determined to see the adventure through in an orderly, methodical way. And she would not turn away from a little fun if it came to her.

She smiled to herself as she recalled Rhys' reaction to Solveig's driving. The icy woman was more to the brothers than the designer of the apartment and the private office at the airport. Clearly she was very familiar to them, especially Tor. The thought of the arrogant man made her back stiffen in the hot water, and she threw off further consideration of the elder Christiansen. When she emerged from the bath, she was met by Inga who wrapped her in a warm, thick towel and led her to a high table. "The quick rub, and then we get you dressed, ya?"

Carol protested—she had never had a massage. She hadn't had anyone fuss over her at all since she was a small child, and certainly not so familiarly as to touch her body. But Inga insisted, so, laughing and accepting, Carol stretched out nervously on the table. In three minutes she felt as though she never wanted to get up. Inga's hands were incredible, strong and gentle at the same time. Soon every inch of her body felt totally relaxed.

"My Tor he says I am as strong as Norse goddess Freya, that I drag the demons out of his body with my hands. That Tor, such a tease he is!"

Carol couldn't imagine Tor teasing anyone about anything, but perhaps it was different with Inga.

"You've known him a long time?"

"Ya, since he was boy. Both him and my Rhys. They are good boys, but Rhys does not eat good. My Tor, he eats like horse!" She was obviously pleased about Tor's eating habits.

Inga's hands had indeed taken the demons out of her body, so much so that she was afraid she would not be able to stand up. But when the woman gave her a final, friendly slap on the behind and helped her up, she felt invigorated and ready to face the evening, whatever it might bring.

"I got dress ready. Pretty."

The dress didn't look too bad, even if she had seen herself in it a thousand times before. The simple lines complemented her slender figure, and the scoop neckline revealed just a hint of the full breasts below.

"You freeze to death!" exclaimed Inga. "I got nice thing you put on shoulders." From a chest of drawers she pulled an elegant woven shawl of soft wool, the pattern a montage of delicately colored threads in pale gold, green and white. Carol draped it over her shoulders and twirled in front of the wall of mirrors. The shawl looked made for the dress.

"It's lovely, Inga!" she said. "Where did it come from?"

"Girl stayed here sometimes, died, very sad. Mrs. Christiansen tells me throw clothes out, but I give away some, keep others. I think some day somebody need, like you! Is good never throw anything away."

Pleased that her saving ways had been totally justified Inga examined her. "Now take hair down and fix. I make coffee."

She left the room without another word. Carol looked at her hair in the mirror. It certainly needed something, but "down"? She brushed it out and stared at it. The color was good, and it had considerable wave in it, but it was so thick and the curls flipped up and around her face with no control whatsoever. Whatever she did, the final effect was one of disarray. Finally, she pinned it back behind her ears, leaving the length of it to wave down her back. It would have to do.

A knock preceeded Inga's voice. "You are ready, ya? They leave soon." Carol opened the door to see a look of disappointment on Inga's face. "They want no coffee! I have whole pot ready!" Apparently the custom of constant coffee was ingrained. Then she smiled, "I take to night watchman downstairs!"

Inga reached out and shook Carol's hand formally. "I go to bed early, so I say good night. Have good time! You wake me up if you need anything."

"Thank you so much for everything, Inga. You've made me feel absolutely wonderful! See you tomorrow." Impulsively, she kissed Inga's rosy cheek and gave her a quick hug. Inga beamed.

There was no need to worry about making an entrance into the living room. Rhys was at the window, staring down at the lights of Oslo in the still-bright day. Solveig and Tor faced away from her at the other end of the room. They seemed deep in an intense conversation that had an edge of argument. Carol didn't feel she could stand at the end of the room and announce her persence, so she quietly joined Rhys at the window.

His eyes swept over her appreciatively. Carol felt very insecure, unused to such blatant perusal, much less admiration. But she took a deep breath and let the warm gaze of Rhys wash over her. It felt very good, that gaze from the blue eyes.

"Little English mouse is no longer so! You are lovely!"

Rhys took her arm and drew her farther from Tor and Solveig, who were so deep in their argument they hadn't seen her. In a conspiratorial tone, Rhys murmured in her ear. "Tor is about to 'put to sea,' as he calls it. He disappears from sight for a few days every once in a while. Solveig does not like to be left behind. But she can plead and argue all night. It will do no good. I hope she gives up soon so we don't have to listen to it all through dinner."

Carol said, lowering her voice also, "Where does he go when he 'puts to sea'?"

"Not really to sea, or Mor, our mother, would be very angry. He has a secret place in the mountains. He meets other trolls there, his mountain trolls, and they get drunk and dance in the night among the wild flowers!"

Carol smiled at the vision. "I envy you your trolls in the mountains. We English must be content with fairies at the bottom of our gardens."

Rhys laughed, delighted that she played his game.

Solveig's voice rose across the room, then hushed itself under Tor's quietly insistent baritone.

Carol asked, "Who is Solveig exactly? She seems so familiar with everything. Is she engaged to Tor?"

Rhys smiled. "She thinks she is. I suppose some day they will marry. It has been expected for many years, since we were all children, even before Joleen."

"Joleen?"

Rhys' voice became hurried, though still casual. "An American girl. Tor met her in the United States, where they attended a seminar together. Her family is very rich, Texas oil. She came here with Tor, her family invested in the company, and she became the unofficial representative of her family's interests. But mostly she played. Joleen played very hard, at everything."

"What happened to her?"

Rhys stiffened. "She died, an accident." Abruptly he grinned and changed the subject. "But you wished to know of Solveig." He began to reel off brand names Carol recognized, a food store shopping list.

"Wait! What have groceries to do with Solveig?"

"They *are* Solveig. They are all her products, marketed under different brand names throughout the common market.

"Solveig's father and ours began a fishing business together many years ago. It was very successful ... many ships and world-wide distribution. When Tor began the drilling operation, he needed capital. Solveig provided much of it. She has made great amounts of money back

35

from the investment, but clearly that isn't all she wants from Tor."

"He doesn't owe her anything then?"

"No, but she trusted him with a great deal of money . . thinking perhaps it was all in the family anyway. But enough of this. We could stand around here all night without a drink. I shall perish if I don't have one soon!"

Without another word, he started across the room and took Solveig by the arm, shouting, "Our lovely visitor from England will faint from hunger if we do not leave at once To the elevator, march!" Solveig was too surprised to protest and submitted to being led away. She scolded Rhys but it was a scolding born of familiarity, without rancor.

Then Tor turned to Carol and the frown that had been on his face for Solveig turned to shock, pain and quickly to fury. Carol could see an angry red spreading along his jaw the muscles tensing. His hand reached up toward the neck of her dress, the fingers posed as though to tear it off Carol could not move, could not even recoil from the threat she felt. But Tor stopped his hand and drew it back controlling whatever urge had thrust it toward her. He looked away from her and shut his eyes tightly for a moment. Then he simply walked away from her toward the elevator where Rhys and Solveig waited for them, both oblivious to what had happened and ended so suddenly

What was wrong with him?! He acted as though he wanted to rip the dress from her body!

Suddenly Carol's heart sank as she remembered casually offered information. It was the shawl. It was Joleen shawl, the Joleen Tor had loved! Of course. How stupid she was! She wanted to rip it from her shoulders hersel But she looked into the foyer where Tor waited calml now. Surely he must understand her blunder had been innocent. Anyway, there was nothing she could do about now. She took a deep breath and joined the others.

Rhys greeted her with an address to all assembled

"Now you see how the ambassador from England looks after just a few hours in Norwegian hands! She is beautiful, ya?"

Carol hastened to take advantage of the opening by saying, "It's this shawl. Inga insisted I wear it. She has been so kind to me."

Solveig interrupted Carol's breathless explanation. "It is quite nice. I see many like them in the nicer shops. But where did it come from?"

Before anyone could offer a theory, Tor said harshly, "It must be Lisle's."

Solveig laughed. "Lisle's? Oh, come now, Tor. Your sister doesn't own anything feminine, much less a piece as elegant as this."

The elevator door opened. Inside, Solveig held forth on current fashions and young people's inattention to that vital matter. But Carol was conscious only of Tor, standing tall and silent so near her, his eyes staring straight ahead. It was going to be a long evening.

Chapter Three

CAROL AND RHYS settled themselves in the back seat of the black and silver BMW sedan, sinking into white leather seats. Tor drove silently, as though he were piloting a jet, Solveig speaking softly in Norwegian beside him. Rhys pointed out main thoroughfares and plazas, and Carol tried to concentrate on his cheerful words. She was struck by the green of the city in the still-light evening of mid-summer. Oslo was so compact compared to London's sprawl. The streets were full of people and the sidewalk cafes were overflowing. Then they passed through the fringes of the city.

"Is the restaurant out in the country?" asked Carol.

"It's more up than out. You'll see in a moment," answered Rhys with a grin.

They parked near a little shed. Rhys helped Carol from the car and pointed toward a tiny cog tram car. Its track aimed up a frighteningly steep incline.

"When I said 'up,' you see I was serious," said Rhys.

"It looks like a toy. Tell me that it's safe," pleaded Carol.

Rhys struck a melodramatic pose. "I cannot lie! It is not safe. We shall probably all crash down the mountain. It happens every day!"

The twenty minute tram ride did not seem real. Carol, who was used to speeding trains and swerving taxi cabs, found this little cog tram with its slow, plodding charm a new experience. It finally sighed to a stop at the top of the mountain.

As they got out, Rhys explained, "This restaurant is the

highest in Oslo. We will have a panoramic view of the city and the fjord."

Carol's eyes scanned the rambling wooden building as they approached it. "It looks centuries old!"

Rhys pointed upwards. "See the dragons?"

Carol looked up at the carved monsters projecting from the roof. She siad, "They look Chinese."

Rhys clutched his heart in horror and groaned. "Chinese?! No! We taught the Chinese everything they know. Those dragons are Viking, little one, *Viking!*" Feeling free and playful, Carol laughed aloud at his antics.

The headwaiter greeted them effusively, especially Solveig, and showed the four of them to a table on the terrace of the restaurant. The view was everything Rhys had promised. Even though it was after eight in the evening, the midnight sun made the whole spectacular landscape glow.

A waiter placed a silver bowl of crushed ice in front of each of them. Nestled in the ice was a heavy crystal glass. As Tor nodded, the waiter produced a bottle encased in a square of ice and poured pale liquid into each glass.

"Aquavit," explained Rhys. "You have to try it."

Carol lifted the icy glass and sipped. "Caraway," she said.

Rhys smiled. "Yes! Take more, and I guarantee you a wonderful time tonight!"

Tor broke his silence with a sharp look at Rhys. "A dangerous guarantee, Rhys, as you know well. A few sips are enough. Aquavit is very strong."

Rhys did not let the challenge drop. "There is no need to protect Carol from a tiny glass of liquor. Controlling *everything* is too big a job for even you, Tor."

As the two brothers locked eyes, Solveig's voice sliced between them to Carol. "It's only right to warn foreigners that all Norwegian customs can't be swallowed at once. Many things are best left to Norwegians."

Rhys raised his glass in a toast. "To Solveig's patriotism and Tor's power! Long may they reign." He swallowed the drink and signaled the waiter to pour another.

Solveig's expression tensed but her voice was smooth and pleasant. "I'm sure that national pride isn't exclusive to Norwegians. I can't believe that the British don't feel protective toward their own. Isn't that right, Miss Smythe?"

They're not talking about customs or patriotism at all, Carol thought. *They're biting at each other through me over old arguments and jealousies and probably that Joleen and this bloody shawl. And if I don't respond, I'll disgrace the Union Jack!* She tried to appear casual as she toyed with her glass and answered, "Of course I'm proud to be British. We have a lot to be proud of. But I feel our greatest history resides in sharing British accomplishments with the world."

Rhys began to hum "Hail Brittania" under his breath. Carol's voice rose over his song. "And we certainly don't view every foreigner as a dangerous intruder."

Solveig's smile was disarming. "I didn't mean to imply that you were in the least dangerous, Miss Smythe."

"I'm not so sure of that," Rhys said, halting his song. He drained his glass, oblivious to the warning Carol could see in Tor's eyes. "Beautiful foreign women bear watching. Never let down your guard, not that you ever have—and not that it ever did you any good."

Carol wanted to shout "Rhys, stop!" She could see that he was moving onto treacherous ground. He didn't seem to care, and the aquavit was giving him courage. Carol knew very little about the American girl who had been part of Tor's life, but she did sense that Rhys was comparing the two of them. And that everyone was uncomfortable. In desperation, Carol managed a nervous giggle and continued with the dinner-table chit-chat.

"No one needs to guard themselves from me. I haven't been sent to infiltrate Norwegian life." She took a deep breath and smiled her most innocent smile. "But I would like to go home with some special stories of Norway. Something unique to make me seem clever. Tell me about this potent aquavit."

Tor broke his silence and reached for the ice-shrouded bottle. "I'll tell you what to do. When you are in a London restaurant with your friends, order aquavit, then peer through the ice and find this stamp." He pointed to a name and date on the label. "Then you say, very casually, 'Did you know this bottle was aged in the hold of this ship as it traveled the South Seas? This date is, of course, the day it crossed the equator. The rolling of the ship is what gives it its mellowness.' Say that, and you will impress one and all with your cosmopolitan knowledge."

"Perfect!" said Carol. "Thank you." Her warm response was the truth, but the story had also successfully detoured the subject to a safer route. And Tor's attention pleased her more than she thought it could after the scene with the shawl. His story was charming, animated and to the point.

Solveig suddenly became solicitous. She rose and reached for Carol's hand. "We must begin on the buffet." She linked her arm with Carol's as though they were old school chums and walked her toward the enormous buffet tables. "Don't let the quantity of food frighten you. I'll guide you through it all."

Carol realized that even sampling everything would result in digestive disaster. She had never seen so much food in one place, and each platter was more beautifully decorated than the one next to it. Solveig continued to be charming. "Our first plate will be just an appetizer. Choose from these platters of herring, then from the smoked eel, then shrimp, then the salmon . . ."

Two hours later, Carol sat back with a satisfied groan. "This is a dangerous country! You don't realize how much you're eating when you keep going back for a new plate every fifteen minutes!"

In spite of the tensions that had marked the beginning of the meal, the quantity and quality of food occupied the conversation and mellowed their mood. With the arrival of a silver coffee pot, they seemed comfortable, pleased with the meal and the justice they had done to it.

Tor looked at Carol over the rim of his coffee cup. "Your position with McKinzie—I'm not sure I understand it. You are Ballinger's assistant, but you say you have no knowledge of the designs."

Carol felt challenged by the quiet words and penetrating eyes. She wasn't ashamed of her job, but she didn't feel she could admit she was essentially a clerk-typist without embarrassing Mr. McKinzie for sending her on this assignment. "I suppose you could say I'm a business apprentice of sorts . . . learning the basic aspects of the entire organization while assigned to Mr. Ballinger." She took a sip of coffee and thought, *There, that should protect me from technical questions. And I haven't actually lied.* It seemed to satisfy Tor, and she breathed a little sigh of relief.

Rhys broke in, "Isn't there a tall Englishman with a bowler hat and a black umbrella who has other plans for you?" His crooked smile was close to a leer.

Carol felt a blush rise on her cheeks and replied with a quiet "No comment." She could hardly discuss a nonexistent lover. Her social life in London was pale indeed. There were several nice young men in the office with whom she had shared a lunch or a film, but these occasions had not grown into even a hint of romance. None of the men, although attentive and pleasant, had touched off any spark. They weren't strong or sure enough. And perhaps they felt the same way about her — after a few evenings, none had pursued her and she didn't consider it especially important, unlike many of the other women in her office. They seemed obsessed with finding a Prince Charming and talked non-stop about the new accountant on the second floor or the handsome salesman visiting from New York. She had her work, and that was enough.

She asked brightly, "Do you have any suggestions for my sightseeing tour of Oslo tomorrow?"

The mention of the weekend made Solveig stiffen visibly and she directed her words to Tor. "Ah, yes, the weekend! Our esteemed host is deserting us all. I suppose I could take you on a short tour."

Rhys said quickly, "Please don't trouble yourself, Solveig. Carol will have my undivided attention for a grand tour."

Tor aborted further discussion by calling for the check, and they made their way to the foyer of the restaurant. Their party was stopped several times on the way, and it was apparent that Miss Folkdahl and the Christiansens were well known. As they chatted with friends, Carol was able to select an assortment of tourist folders from the front desk and place them neatly in her handbag. With that wealth of printed information in her possession, there would be no need to ask anyone about sightseeing possibilities.

On the tram ride down the mountain, Carol was fascinated to glimpse a huge ski jump on a distant hill. She was terribly proud of herself for recognizing it and said, "That's the famous Holmenkollen Jump, isn't it? The ski jump competition—I always watch it on the telly—it's my favorite Olympic event."

Rhys waved his hand toward his brother, saying, "I defer to Tor, who is the rider in the family. He can tell you more than you'd ever want to know about that hill."

Carol felt like a little girl suddenly confronted with a favorite film star. "Really? You've jumped off that hill?"

"No more," he answered tersely. "Riding the Holmenkollen is something you do when you are young and foolish."

"I would love to hear about it . . ." She let the sentence

trail off, realizing that Tor didn't want to discuss the ski jump. Carol was genuinely disappointed. She vowed to find another time to introduce the subject. She really wanted to know what it felt like to fly down that frightening incline and soar off into thin air ... and what kind of man would dare to do it.

The luxurious car purred toward the center of the city. Carol stared at the back of Tor's head, her mind preoccupied with visions of flying men on skis.

Tor addressed them all. "It will be most efficient if I drop you off first, Rhys ... then Solveig. I'll see Miss Smythe safely to the apartment, then pick up my things and be on my way out of town."

Rhys protested, "We must have a nightcap! You're the only one, Tor, who has a long drive ahead of you."

Tor's voice was stern. "Your idea of a nightcap can go on for hours. Turn in early and save the parties for tomorrow. Miss Smythe is tired."

Carol wasn't in the least tired, but she couldn't object to Tor Christiansen's judgment. She was surprised that Rhys had no reply. He merely slouched down in the seat and sulked. The car halted in front of an older building where each bow-windowed apartment had its own flower box, so all four stories seemed to be in bloom. Rhys opened his door.

"Rhys," said Tor, "I'll leave the car keys with Miss Smythe for your use tomorrow. Good night."

Rhys grunted his understanding of his instructions, got out of the car and turned back to Carol. "I'll call you around nine o'clock in the morning to make arrangements." He slammed the door and started toward his apartment building.

The car started moving away. Carol looked out the rear window to see Rhys turn sharply away from the building and hail a passing taxi. *So much for his turning in early,* she thought.

44

Solveig was speaking to Tor in an undertone. "So, Tor, what am I going to do about the Jorgensen's dinner party on Thursday? Can I count on your being there or must I make apologies for you?"

The words of his answer were measured, as though he had said them many times before. "I have no idea how long business will keep me in Bergen. Much depends on what Miss Smythe has brought from London and what stage of development it is in. There may be problems in Stavanger. I haven't been out on the rig for several weeks. My return must be kept open."

"Open? That's not good enough, Tor." There was no attempt to keep the conversation private. "Astrid Jorgensen is planning on us. We must let her know. Promise me you'll be here."

Carol could see Tor's jaw jut forward. He said evenly, "I'll call you when my schedule clears."

Tor swung into the circular drive of a large, modern building. A uniformed doorman leapt to attention, and Solveig was ushered out of the car as if she were royalty. Without a word or a backward glance, she walked through the glass doors and disappeared.

Perhaps she is royalty, thought Carol. *She acts as though she expects everyone to bow.* And the doorman had.

Tor turned to her. "Miss Smythe, perhaps you would like to move to the front seat? You can see the city more easily, and I won't feel like your chauffeur."

Carol dutifully made the switch.

"You must fasten your seat belt. In Norway it is the law, and it is strictly enforced."

She fumbled for the belt and couldn't find the secret of latching it. The harder she tried, the more tangled the shoulder harness became. Tor reached across her body and methodically straightened the strap and pulled it firmly across her breasts. His strong square hands were over hers, guiding them against the metal clasp. The lock engaged under her hands and she looked up to say "Thank you," conscious that he had not released her hands. She saw his face close to hers, his eyes shadowed and unreadable. She found his nearness overwhelming, and no words came. His eyes seemed to be searching hers from his own shadows, and his hands tightened on hers. Carol sat very still, sensing his warmth, his breath, the intense current between them. After a long moment, Tor gave a quick shake of his head and drew away.

Perhaps the moment hadn't been as long as she thought. Carol found her voice and said, "Thank you, Mr. Christiansen. I'm usually not so awkward about mechanical things."

"You are most welcome, Miss Smythe." He turned to the wheel.

It was a short distance to the apartment, and though Carol stared intently at the passing scene, she saw nothing. Tor's shadowed face filled her field of vision, and she still felt the heat of his hands on her own. The intensity of her feelings frightened her.

As he parked the car and they ascended to the penthouse, his conversation was polite and distant. "I will leave you the keys to the apartment, and here is a set of keys to the BMW. Rhys has some, but he will undoubtedly misplace them at a critical moment."

"Thank you. You are very generous."

"Not at all. You must enjoy your stay in our country."

Carol took part in the formal dialogue as though she were watching herself in a play. The words burning in her mind, the ones she wanted to say, were "Who are you? Why do you make me feel this way?" She wanted to sit down and talk to this man for days, to ask him all the important questions and all the silly ones.

But they were moving into the penthouse foyer, and Inga was waiting.

"Home so early, ya? Such a handsome couple! You are hungry, ya? I fix little snack."

Tor answered for both of them. "No, Inga, we have just eaten our way through about fifty kilos of food."

"For you, my Tor, just an appetizer!" Inga gestured toward a huge wicker hamper on the floor of the foyer. "This is your food basket of the weekend. I never know how much to put in because it always comes back empty." Inga put her hand on Carol's arm and confided, "This boy has such good appetite."

The sight of the hamper seemed to mobilize Tor, and he began to reel off instructions. "Inga, I don't know when I will be back in Oslo. Don't look for me for at least a week." He stripped off his jacket and loosened his tie, formality forgotten as he hurried. "You can fly to Bergen if I stay for any length of time. Mor and Grete would like to have you for a while, I'm sure. I'm taking the MG. Excuse me while I change."

As he hurried down the hall, Inga called after him, "You want coffee before you leave, ya?"

"Always, Inga, always." And he was gone.

Carol hesitated. Perhaps she should go to her room and get out of the way. She knew she should be tired, but instead she felt strangely energetic and didn't want the day to end just yet. Inga ended her hesitation by propelling her toward the kitchen. Carol was soon busy finding mugs and setting the table for "a little snack." She felt so comfortable with Inga, and she was pleased that Inga apparently felt the same way with her.

Soon Tor reappeared, striding into the kitchen. Carol hardly recognized him. Gone was the severe business executive, and in his place stood a Viking. Oh, there was no shaggy animal skin or horned helmet, but the man was so tall, so blond and tan, and his manner so free and daring. Sturdy hiking boots and heavy corduroy pants were topped by a ski jersey and the most magnificent sweater Carol had ever seen.

Carol stilled the tiny quiver in her stomach and man-

47

aged to exclaim, "That sweater! I've never seen anything like it!"

Tor slipped the cardigan off his shoulders and tossed it to her. The weight of the wool stunned her. She explored the intricate white pattern knit into the black wool, and touched the heavy pewter clasps. "This weighs more than I do," she said, and handed it back to him.

"It also tells a story," said Tor. "The pattern tells what district of Norway you come from, much like the plaids of Scotland define clan."

"It seems so heavy for late spring."

"Not in the mountains. The air at night is cold. There is still snow."

Carol watched Tor consume coffee and a mountain of cookies as Inga chattered at him, her voice musical and motherly. Slowly the hard edges of Tor seemed to soften, and once Carol thought she saw the hint of a smile on his face.

Satisfied that Tor would be able to survive now, with his stomach full, Inga stood up and announced, "Is past the time for my bed. You drive the mountain careful, Tor." She patted his arm, beamed at both of them, and went out of the kitchen.

With Inga gone, with the two of them alone, everything seemed to change. Carol's mouth felt dry, her throat tight, and she stared at the cookie in her hand. She had no idea what to say to the man across the table.

He spoke finally, and his voice seemed strained. "I want to apologize for the dinner tonight. Our manners were very bad, and we were not gracious. It must have been uncomfortable for you."

"Please don't feel that way." Carol wanted to meet his eyes, but he stared off into some distance she could not fathom. "It was a lovely restaurant, and a meal that I'll never forget."

"Rhys and Solveig are not good together. So much history among us all." He said this as fact, not inviting either question or observation.

Suddenly Carol began to feel the fatigue that was inevitable after a day such as she had spent. She fought it, wanting the day to end with some kind of definition. She wanted a finish as clean and neat as her desk at the end of a working day.

"Somehow I feel responsible for the . . . tension at dinner," she said. Tor looked at her sharply, but she went on, determined to clear matters up. "I think I was a catalyst that upset each of you in some way. It certainly wasn't my intention . . . but right from the beginning . . . the shawl . . . but Inga was so concerned that I might be cold, and by the time I realized that it once belonged to . . ."

A steel curtain dropped over his eyes. "Possibly therapy is more your area of expertise than marine engineering, but it is not necessary."

Carol felt as though she had been slapped. She had reached out to him in a caring way, as much for him as for herself, and had been thrust away. Her spine stiffened against the chair. "Surely you have more important things to do than comment on my myriad faults!"

He rose suddenly, the chair screeching back as he pushed it aside. A rush of fear went through Carol as she recalled Rhys' comment on his brother's violent temper, but the hard words were controlled, formal. "I'm taking Ballinger's material with me. Enjoy your weekend. I will expect you in Bergen Monday."

Carol looked at him, expecting an abrupt exit, a slamming door. But he stood there, staring at her. The voice of her mind said to him, *Go please! Drive to your mountain and leave me alone*! But she said nothing.

He picked up his sweater and folded it over his arm. He stared down at it and then laughed—a short, humorless laugh. "Perhaps someday we can compare your myriad faults to mine. I'm sure mine would more than equal yours." Then he turned and left the room quickly.

Carol sat very still. Was than an apology or not? She felt incomprehensible tears rising in her eyes and fought them back. She was not the kind of woman who wept over every little thing, even the frustrating confusion she felt now. She could hear the sounds of Tor's activity, abrupt and angry movements, in another part of the apartment. Then a door slammed and there was silence.

She forced herself out of the chair and attacked the dishes, clearing the table and then scrubbing everything in a compulsive fury. The table was wiped and polished to a shine, the coffee pot scoured within an inch of its life, and the cookies were sealed away in a brightly painted tin. During her work she didn't allow herself to think or feel anything.

Closing her bedroom door, she saw her reflection in the wall of mirrors. Her hair was disheveled, its copper highlights failing to either flatter or disguise the flush in her face and the redness around her eyes. The dress was wrinkled and showed its age. She looked like a sad little English waif, which was exactly how she felt, weak and completely out of her element of order and discipline. She felt the tears coming as she carefully folded the shawl and put it in a drawer, never wanting to see it again. Habit made her remove and carefully hang up her clothes. She put on her soft cotton nightgown with tears streaming down her face. She felt absolutely ridiculous, blew her nose and settled into the bed, vowing to pull herself together.

A quiet tap sounded on her door, and Inga's round face appeared as it opened a crack. "There is something you need, ya?" The sympathetic eyes looked into Carol's, and the tears started afresh.

Carol clenched her fists as Inga came into the room and sat down on the bed. "No, Inga, there's nothing I need. I'm afraid I'm going to make a terrible botch of everything, and I think your Tor is the rudest man I've ever met and I want to please him far too much and I don't understand him or myself . . ."

Inga began to massage Carol's shoulders and neck gently as the words tumbled out. The warm hands seemed to take the pain away and Carol relaxed into them. Inga began to croon softly, as though to a child. "Ya, I see something of what goes on. But you do not worry. Tor is very bad sometimes. Is not happy man, and you see that, ya? Is two years since his girl, Joleen, die. He still hurt bad. Need time, my Tor does. No one can help him yet . . . is so cold. But I see different look in eyes tonight. I think you mix him up. Good. He needs mix up."

"I'm not trying to mix him up, Inga. I'm just trying to get along with him. But he mixes me up, and that frightens me! I can't sort it out at all. This morning I had never thought about Norway or Folkdahl or Christiansen. Rhys called this an 'adventure.' Some adventure!"

"You just tired. Too much in one day. Midsummer time fools everyone, forget to sleep. You sleep now. Tomorrow is new time under sun. You will see our city, enjoy. I will make fresh coffee cake for breakfast."

Carol began to sink into the sleep Inga promised. The gentle lady tucked her in under the soft coverlet, turned off the lights and left the room. Carol sank further into sleep, thinking *This bed is delicious, and whatever else . . .*

That was the last thought she had that night.

Chapter Four

CAROL AWOKE WITH an awareness of sunlight all around her. She sat up, instantly awake, and knew that it was late. In the clear morning light, the dark and confusing thoughts were gone from her mind. Her crying spell of the night before seemed foolish, and she put it down to fatigue. She felt rested and alive. After a quick, refreshing shower, she grabbed a robe to go in search of Inga.

The center of the kitchen table held a banquet and a note: "I go visit friend in hospital. Gall bladder, not bad. Eat breakfast. Inga."

Carol's eye caught the clock — 9:30! Had she slept through Rhys' promised call? Her search through the Oslo telephone book listed only one "Rhys Christiansen." She dialed and waited while it rang to no avail. Finally she abandoned the instrument and went back to her room to dress.

In less than thirty minutes she was in comfortable clothes and walking shoes, had done some justice to the breakfast that Inga had set out for her, and was on her second cup of coffee with guide books of Oslo spread out in front of her. Several more attempts to call her guide had proved fruitless, and she resolved not to wait any longer. She made a decision to take a ferry to Bygdoy, a suburb of Oslo on a peninsula. According to the brochures, Bygdoy contained a marvelous collection of things to see and do on a summer day. As she gathered her things together, preparing to set off alone, she wondered, *Would I wait longer if Tor had promised to be my guide*? She dismissed the thought, descended in the leather elevator, and stepped out into the warm and welcome sunshine. She felt an enormous sense of freedom and independence.

A perfect day for a boat ride, she decided, and set off in the direction of the ferry boats to Bygdoy. Mentally, she ticked off her itinerary. She was pleased with her orderly, logical plan: the Folk Museum, the Viking ships, and the *Kon Tiki.*

The boat for Bygdoy was crowded with excited tourists and families on an outing. The sun, the clean air, and the wheeling gulls overhead made the mini-cruise all too short.

Stop number one, she thought, *is the Viking Ship Museum. I've certainly 'done' enough British museums to know what to expect.* She stepped through the main doors and froze. This wasn't a museum—it was a church! The plain white plaster walls rose to a vaulted ceiling, stark and dramatic. From the flagstone floor rose the *Oseburg.* The Viking ship was awesome, not in its size, but in its graceful strength — its sweeping lines and jutting prow took her breath away. Carol experienced one of those rare moments when one feels both a part of and separate from history. *A thousand years ago,* Carol thought, *they sailed ships like these to invade and conquer England. My ancestors lived in fear of these very ships. They must have seen these prows, these rearing sea serpents, coming out of the mist to land on England's shores.* She thought of the carved Latin motto hung in the dusty display cabinet at the office—"From the Norsemen's fury, deliver us, Oh Lord"—and she thought of Tor Christiansen.

Unlike the museums Carol was familiar with, this was very uncluttered and plain. Only three boats existed, and they alone were displayed here. There was nothing to distract one from the ships. She walked around each several times, absorbing the intricate carvings, then moved on from the ship museum to the building that housed the

Kon Tiki. This was not ancient history, and Carol remembered reading about it and seeing films of its voyage. She knew Thor Heyerdahl had sailed the balsa raft from Peru to Polynesia, but she was not prepared for what confronted her. *It's so frail, so fragile. It looks incapable of floating across an English pond.* Carol shivered. *It wasn't only the ancient Vikings who were fearless.*

She decided to explore the outdoor Folk Museum nearby. From her morning reading, she knew that it was a microcosm of the folkways, traditions and buildings of Norway. *What a pleasant way to tour a museum,* she thought, *out of doors in the June sunshine.* She started to move into the area when the idea of food became paramount. Consulting her guidebook, she found that the Museum Restaurant had a high rating as a "beautifully decorated building with open-air dining." She needed no further convincing.

Carol chose an outdoor table near the folk dance stage and ordered cold salmon with dill and a salad. The table was a communal one, but she was its only occupant. She was about to settle into her solitary meal when a friendly American voice asked, "Are all these places taken?" She turned to see a group of young people waiting for her answer.

"No, please sit down."

The young man deployed his friends around the table. Carol was suddenly surrounded by an international flock of students all of whom seemed to be talking to her at once in a dozen different languages. The American shouted, "Hey, you guys! Remember, I found her first. Finders keepers, losers weepers! Go ahead and weep."

"You found me?" asked Carol. "And I didn't even know I was lost! You Americans are so quick to make property claims!"

"Yankee ingenuity! We learned it all from you British! Let me introduce you all around your table."

Carol could not begin to remember all the names and countries represented, but she estimated seven nationalities and a wide variety of interests, enthusiasms and opinions. Halfway through her salmon, Carol felt completely at ease with them.

How easy it is to talk to strangers, she mused and wondered why they were paying her so much pleasant attention—perhaps she wasn't a *mus* at all.

Everyone began to compare and compete with touring plans for the coming week. With a strange new sense of freedom, Carol found herself saying clever things, joining their laughter, leading the conversation. *I'd never be doing this at home,* she marveled *But in a fresh, new place, where no one knows me, I can be anyone I want—a whole new me. Or perhaps the real me can come out.* It was an exhilarating thought.

Carol launched into the story of her flight, her passport and Mrs. Pickett, then her trip to Bergen on Monday. "So I'll fly to Bergen and ..."

A groan went up around the table.

"What's the matter?" asked Carol, a little worried about their collective reaction. "Is something wrong with Bergen?"

"Don't fly!"

"That's the most spectacular drive."

"You'll miss all the mountain scenery."

"The waterfalls, the gorges, the fjords!"

"Stop!" said Carol, covering her ears. "Don't tempt me! The plans are all made. I'm here for business, not pleasure, and I'll be horribly depressed if I think about what I'm missing."

The American would not be deterred. "Promise us that you'll try to see some of it all before you leave Norway."

"I have no idea what I'll be able to do. My guide has a real talent for disappearing."

"Then count on me! I would never pull a disappearing

act on someone like you. Dump him, and let's do an English pub-crawl through Oslo tonight!"

From across the table, a swarthy young Italian with enormous black eyes reached for her hand. "If this 'pub-crawling' is not your cup of the English tea, allow me to offer myself to you. Your every wish will be my command." He caressed the palm of her hand delicately.

"You're all very sweet, but I don't want to break up your happy group. We might all go together." Carol disengaged her hand and smiled, feeling a bit like an older aunt. They were the same age, but they were students while she was a working woman. It made a difference.

Their conversation halted with the appearance of the folk dancers, and for half an hour the swirling colors of the costumes and the beat of the music had them clapping their hands and pounding their feet. At the end of the dances, Carol was very much a part of their group, and they all set out together for the Folk Museum.

The afternoon seemed to skim by, and at 5:00 the museum personnel began to move them toward the ferry boats and Oslo. Carol and her new friends stood along the rail of the boat, looking at the hundreds of craft in the Oslo harbor. Everywhere one looked, there was a different kind of boat, each delicately balanced in the deep blue water.

The young men were being very attentive, and Carol was very flattered. She found herself laughing as much as they were as they played a hopeless game of counting sails. Then Carol glanced toward the bow of the ferry and saw a familiar profile. Could it be Rhys? She moved to get a better view. There was no doubt—Rhys was draped against the rail, dressed in exactly the same clothes he had worn the night before! He looked terrible.

He can't be sea-sick, she decided. *The harbor is as calm as a lake. I'm looking at a man with a monumental hangover. He hasn't even been home. No wonder no one answered the telephone this morning.* Her initial reaction was to ignore him, but the more she thought about it, the angrier she became. She said to the Italian student, "My disappearing guide has suddenly materialized. There he is, sagging on the rail."

"You want me to throw him overboard?"

"No, thank you. I think I will handle this myself. Excuse me." And she walked briskly toward Rhys.

"Mr. Christiansen! What a surprise! Have you been visiting the museums?" As Rhys turned to face her, his blood-shot eyes strained to focus. "Imagine bumping into you here! I didn't know you spent your Saturdays looking at thirteenth century churches."

He was embarrassed, and Carol felt a certain satisfaction at knowing he had that much sensitivity.

"Carol, I don't know how to begin to apologize . . ."

"There's no need to apologize. I have had a wonderful day, met charming people, and seen more Norwegian history and tradition than I can begin to digest. I've done very well without your esteemed company."

He fumbled about for a reply. "You see, things got very complicated . . . I had some other commitments . . . I . . ."

"I am not one of your commitments. You needn't feel at all responsible for me, Rhys. I've taken good care of myself all day, and I intend to continue doing so."

"But I *am* responsible for you. Tor made it very clear . . ."

"I see. Tor decides everything. Let me relieve you of the burden. I'm not a tattle-tale and won't report you to your big brother."

Carol turned to leave, but Rhys put his hand on her arm. His voice was quiet but insistent. "I'm glad you've had a good day, and I'm sorry you didn't have it with me. Let me show you Oslo at night."

The boat was docking, and Carol's new friends were calling for her to join them. The Italian viewed Rhys with suspicion. She started to shake off Rhys' hand.

"Please, Carol." The plea in his voice weakened her resolve. He seemed as repentant as a little boy.

As the crowd disembarked from the ferry, Carol explained to her friends that, although their plans of an evening hike in the hills sounded wonderful, she was a city girl with sore feet. She promised to call their hotel tomorrow if she were free. She left them with a warm wave and a sense of disappointment, knowing she would probably never see any of them again.

Rhys was at her side as she left the harbor and walked toward the grand city hall.

"Are you hungry, Carol? There are good restaurants in this area."

"I had a very late lunch, thank you."

"Good. I'm not ready to eat, either. And that leaves us time for shopping."

"Shopping? For what?"

"Now before you get all prickly, let me explain that this is a legitimate responsibility." He was digging in his wallet, and he produced a chit on North Sea Petroleum letterhead. "See this? My big brother gave orders. He feels we threw you on a plane with no notice, and now we are demanding that you stay here for at least a week. You had no chance to pack properly or get ready for anything. This shopping spree, little mouse, is on the company."

"What am I supposed to buy?"

His laugh was loud and genuine. "Anything you want!"

Rhys steered her into a gleaming, smart shop. Carol had no time to dwell on the surprising thoughfulness of Tor. It was true that she had nothing with her but the skirt and blouse she had on, one dress and the gray suit. "Perhaps I might get something for work in the Bergen office," she said.

In the next two hours, Carol discovered another side of Rhys. He had excellent, as well as extravagant, taste. As they went from shop to shop, Rhys went through racks with a quick, unerring eye, pulled and pointed, and entertained her and every shop girl in Oslo with his charm and delight in the task. Carol protested his extravagance to no avail until the bags and boxes rose up to his chin.

"This is all, Rhys! We just can't justify any more. We're going home."

In the excitement of shopping, the tension between Rhys and Carol had evaporated. She had not forgotten that he was irresponsible, but she had just accepted that as part of his character. *If you don't rely on him, just accept him for what he is, things are quite pleasant,* she thought. *I'm just going to enjoy him.*

Arriving at the apartment, Rhys handed her all the parcels and propelled himself to the sofa. He mumbled something about "a little nap." In an instant he was sound asleep, curled up like a very tall little boy.

Carol took her bundles to her room and began to open each one, reveling in the best part of shopping—coming home and looking at everything.

Once she had each item arranged on the bed, Carol stepped back and was amazed at the choices. She would never have selected such an array in London even if she could have spent the money. There she tended toward severe city colors that were as utilitarian and as neutral as the surroundings. What she saw before her were the soft textures and bold colors of Scandinavia. She had never seen such purity of color—reds so rosy, blues so deep, yellows so vibrant. The solid colors of the full cotton skirts could mix and match with the geometrics and flowers of the blouses. Several short cotton jackets pulled the wardrobe together. The parcels even contained some surprises. Rhys had added items that she had dismissed as too frivolous. She now owned a mini dress that Rhys described as "New Wave Disco," and bright green hiking overalls complete with bib and suspenders. *That would cause some comment in the office.* She giggled at the thought, and wondered where in the world she would ever wear them. But her favorite of the surprises was a sweater of purest white with russet and deep blue hearts knit in a subtle design around the full rolled collar. She couldn't resist trying it on. As she fastened the pewter clasps and felt the soft wool cuddling her, she was grateful to Rhys. The gifts were fun and thoughtful. *How can I stay angry at him?* she asked herself. *He's like a naughty little boy who feels badly about his mischief. But that doesn't mean he won't do it again.*

Carol carefully put away her new purchases, taking special care with the sweater. Once the bed was cleared, it invited her insistently. It had been a full day, and she wasn't used to being outdoors in the fresh air and sun. She took off her shoes, fell onto the bed, and immediately dropped off to sleep.

A tapping on her door awakened her. Rhys' voice was full of demanding energy. "Carol! Let's go! The revels commence!"

Carol roused herself sleepily. "Revels? Oh, Rhys, I don't think I can move!"

Rhys began a resounding tenor version of a popular disco tune and beat out the rhythm with loud thumps of his fists on her door. She shouted over the din, "All right! Give me twenty minutes!"

"Twenty minutes, the absolute limit, ya?" he shouted through the door. "You put on the little bitty dress! I shall die with anticipation!

Carol rushed to shower and change. She brushed her thick hair and decided to let it hang loose around her shoulders. *It doesn't look like me,* she thought, *but I'm weary of looking like me.*

Rhys shouted again through her door, "Twenty minutes is up! Come out immediately!"

Carol stood up and glanced at her image in the wall of mirrors. The dress was awfully short, and Carol had moment of doubt. But her legs were her best feature, and the dress did look nice, if she did say so herself. The emerald jersey had a scooped neck and long, tight sleeves, and a dropped waist that held a tiny gathered skirt. She felt a bit insecure as she went out of the bedroom, but if this was what one wore on a date with Rhys Christiansen, so be it.

Rhys was slouched against the wall right outside the door, his impatient look immediately changing to a broad, appreciative grin when he saw her. He had changed from his rumpled suit into tight black corduroy slacks, and a cotton turtle-neck of deep blue-green.

"You've changed clothes, too!"

"I've been home and have returned to claim my prize." He straightened up with a long, low whistle. "And what a prize! Turn around!"

She obeyed, her color rising as his admiring gaze went over her from head to foot. She wished he would utter the obligatory compliment and get it over with, but his examination continued. Finally, she said, "I've never been so exposed at such great expense."

"You look marvelous! And more covered up than I would like at this moment."

He stepped in close to her and touched the soft fabric of the dress at the neckline, as though to adjust the curve of it. She felt his warm hand move over her shoulder and to the back of her neck.

"The little English mouse has disappeared, and a most lovely creature has taken its place."

"Rhys . . ." she began, but he gently laid a finger across her lips and spoke softly in Norwegian as he pulled her close to him, words she didn't know but could understand. His face was buried in her neck and hair, moving gently as he murmured the sweet sounds. Carol drew back but he held her head in his hands and looked into her eyes.

"Carol, lovely green-eyed Carol . . ."

It wasn't right, and Carol felt her common sense returning. She pulled away from him and said, "I'm very flattered, Rhys, but we really don't know each other well . . ."

"We know all there is to know." He held her shoulders.

"I don't want to fight, Rhys. Forget about all this. Let's just go out and have a good time. Please." Her voice was firm and drew a clear line between them.

He was silent for an eternity, looking down at her intently, longingly. She returned his gaze unwaveringly.

Finally, a small sigh escaped his lips. "For an ex-mouse, you drive a hard bargain. I accept your terms, but I don't like them."

"Do we have a deal?" asked Carol.

"Deal."

"Good. Thank you for being a gentleman."

Rhys didn't answer. Some of the energetic, bantering tone came back into his voice as he started toward the kitchen. "Come quick with me! You are fortunate. I have a surprise!"

She followed him, feeling as though she had won a small victory. "Another surprise? What?"

"It is Inga's night off! And you have the honor to be served by Rhys Christiansen, the chef supreme!"

Inga's table was littered with chunks and bits and piles of food. The chaos was a travesty of Inga's idea of setting out a meal and of the Norwegian sense of order and decoration. She laughed and Rhys beamed.

"You laugh, ma'am? You do not see that I fulfill my penchant for clutter and cuteness? Sit!" He pulled a chair out for her. "This way we do not waste time in a restaurant when we can be dancing."

Carol sat down. "If I weren't sure that Inga made all this, I'd hesitate. You've managed to smear everything over everything!" Carol ate hungrily. Rhys watched her, occasionally offering a comment on the incredible appetite of English mice. He ate little and was impatient when she insisted on clearing away the debris.

"Anyone who looks as you do should not perform domestic service! I will have to protect you from the Nordic hordes tonight."

There was still some tension between them, but they both seemed to be determined to make the best of the evening ahead of them.

Carol had been to discotheques in London, and she correctly assumed they were the same the world over—flashing lights, blaring music, and a dance floor crowded with young people dressed for fun and show. What she was not prepared for was the reception accorded Rhys. Not a dance went by that several people did not interrupt to say hello or ask them to join their party. Rhys was an obvious favorite with women, and the men tolerated his attentions to their dates without rancor. *And I imagine that the Christiansen name has an effect, too,* thought Carol. Rhys danced hard and drank with equal intensity. The more he drank, the more loquatious and convivial he became toward everyone but Carol. She found herself in a great mob of people, all familiar with each other, all shouting anecdotes and private jokes in English for her benefit but meaningless all the same.

She danced herself into exhaustion with a dozen beautiful men. But Rhys was less and less in evidence. Finally, she made her way through a group that surrounded him and shouted over the pulsing beat of the music.

"Rhys, how much longer will we be staying?"

He laughed over the din and made an attempt to focus on her. "They will have to close the place around us! Everyone is here tonight. You are having fun, ya?" Abruptly he wheeled away from her to embrace another group that had just discovered him.

Carol found herself being steered to an empty table away from the bar by a Viking prince whose name she didn't catch.

"Rhys has wonderful taste in women. Do you have to go home with him tonight?"

"I wasn't planning on it."

"Then you and I can make plans."

"No, you and I are not going to make plans." She fended off his, and several others', advances with surprising facility. Resentment was building in her. *Rhys has some responsibility toward me and, at this moment, he has no idea where I am.* She didn't want to start any arguments but decided it was time to pry Rhys away from the bar and go back to the apartment.

"Excuse me," Carol said as she tapped him on the shoulder. "This English Cinderella hears the clock tolling the witching hour. Could my carriage take me home?" She sweetened her request with a big smile and playful curtsy.

Her effort at pleasantness was not returned. He barely glanced at her, his eyes bleary and unfocused, while he signaled for refills all around.

"Please, Rhys," Carol said more sharply, "I'd like to leave."

"Go ahead. Little mouse is free to crawl into her mouse-hole. I will not stop you."

"Good! Where can I get a taxi?"

He dug into his pocket and brought out the car keys. He dangled them in front of her nose. "No need to get a taxi. Drive the car home. I'm feeling too good to drive anything." An angry note sounded through his drunken slur. "Tor's car will be safe with you. You are sober like a judge."

She caught the keys as he dropped them and was about to protest when he turned away and began to converse with a tall, buxom girl at the bar.

Just like that, fumed Carol, *he drops the keys in my*

hand and me out of his head. So be it. I can find the apartment easily enough, if I can just find my way out of this chaos!

She retrieved the BMW from the parking lot and drove back to the apartment. The car was incredible, and her anger quickly dissipated as the machine responded to her commands. *It doesn't have the personality of my little Morris,* she concluded, *but that's not exactly a disadvantage*!

As the elevator deposited her at the penthouse door, she was simply disappointed that the evening had ended on such an unpleasant note. She turned the key in the lock and heard the phone ringing deep within the apartment. As she stepped into the foyer, the persistent ring continued. After a momentary hesitation, she recalled the phone on Tor's office desk and ran toward it.

"Hello," she said breathlessly, "Tor Christiansen's office. Carol Smythe speaking. May I help you?" Her answering phrase was automatic, and she hoped the caller spoke English.

"This is Tor Christiansen, Miss Smythe."

Carol's breath stilled as she heard his voice.

"I have unpacked the briefcase you brought from London and cannot find a file on wave dynamics. I know there was one."

"Yes, I remember it, Mr. Christiansen. I'm in your office now. Let me look around." Carol threw on every light switch in the room, and her eye immediately went to the missing folder. "It's right here on your desk."

"It does me no good there. Find Rhys. Tell him to get in the car and bring me that folder in Geilo. He is to meet me for breakfast at six o'clock at the Stenlund Lodge with that file in his hand."

"Now? Tonight?" Carol was not sure she had heard correctly. She was supposed to track down Rhys and put him in a car with the file? It was impossible. "I . . . I doubt that Rhys will be able to . . ."

"I want that file by six o'clock in the morning. If he's drunk, pour coffee down his throat."

"But he's . . ."

"Please take care of it, Miss Smythe."

The line went dead and Carol slowly replaced the receiver. Rhys wouldn't listen to her even if she went back to the disco, and by now he might have gone to another bar. In any case, he was in no condition to drive to Geilo. Even Norwegian coffee couldn't work miracles. He was in no condition to drive around the block.

As she stood beside the desk, Carol felt the weight of the car keys in her hand. "Where is that map?" she asked herself aloud and headed toward her bedroom. She pulled the road map from the pile of brochures and opened it. The name "Geilo" sprang out at her on a main road, about halfway between Oslo and Bergen. Her rough calculation indicated that the distance from Oslo was about 200 kilometers, just a few hours' drive. And the idea of driving the BMW out into the countryside . . . She threw open her suitcase and began throwing her clothes into it. One more adventure, and Tor Christiansen would have his precious file.

Inga's voice at the door stopped her preparations. "Where are you going in that tiny little dress?" Inga was wrapped in a huge flannel robe. She looked sleepy and confused. "Such a dress. You will catch your death!"

Carol looked down at herself. "True! I'm going to change into some comfortable slacks. I must take this file to Tor in Geilo. I can't wait to drive that car again!"

Inga protested, "You are mixed up! You not drive to Gielo. You go by fly to Gielo! Come and have coffee."

"Coffee is a wonderful idea, Inga. Do you have a thermos? It would be marvelous to have a thermos of coffee and a few cookies on the drive! Would you mind? I'm in a bit of a hurry."

Poor Inga had become even more upset after Carol had

insisted on her spontaneous plan, standing up to every argument the worried lady listed: "You not used to left-hand drive, the road too dangerous, there are trolls in mountains," and Carol was too tired, too little, too everything.

Nevertheless, a huge thermos of coffee was now perched on the seat beside her, and a huge bag of cookies accompanied it. *If I can stand up to Inga,* she thought triumphantly, *I can stand up to anyone.*

As she eased the car onto the wide street, Carol was sure Inga was over-reacting to the whole situation. After all, it was as bright as day, she was an excellent driver, and the map was very clear. It would be just like driving from London to Nottingham. What could possibly go wrong?

Chapter Five

CAROL HAD NEVER stayed up all night in her life. But she wasn't in the least tired, and this night was as light as day. The clean, fresh air invigorated her. She breathed deeply of it and sensed its coolness on her skin. *I'm going to keep the windows rolled down all the way to Geilo, until every bit of London dust is out of my lungs!* She wondered what Rhys would say when he found out about this impromptu trip. *I think he would call it another virgin adventure and applaud loudly,* Carol thought, and she smiled to herself.

The petrol gauge read "full," and the engine roared wonderfully. She had never driven a car so powerful, so elegant. The left-hand drive felt strange, but she knew she would get used to it quickly. After a few adjustments, the leather seat fit her perfectly, and her hands felt light and strong on the sensitive steering wheel. She accelerated slowly, testing the car's reactions and her own, and began to enjoy the power under her and her own power over it.

The light enhanced the buildings of Oslo, giving them a life of their own in the almost-empty streets. Her gaze lifted to the western horizon, and a tiny quiver of anxiety tremored across her shoulders. She had never driven in mountains before, and it was a strange road. *What if something happens to me at almost one o'clock in the morning in a strange country? And I don't speak the language? And what am I doing here, about to confront a man who attracts and repels me—on a mountaintop in the wilds of Norway?* Carol shook the questions from her mind. *If I keep asking myself frightening questions, I'll end up turn-*

*ing the car around and running home to Inga . . . virgin
adventure missed! I know what I'm doing.*

It was only a matter of minutes before she reached the
edge of the city and started into the mountains. The road
seemed very narrow for a major thoroughfare between
two cities, and it was climbing with breathtaking rapidity.
"I'm not going to run into any difficulties." She voiced the
hope aloud. "I am going to arrive in plenty of time and
enjoy the scenery along the way. What do you know? I'm
an international traveler!" She had tasted independence,
and it was delicious. *I've been far too content to travel
from my flat to the office, with small detours to the cinema.
With perhaps just a small raise in pay, I could make a trip
every year, somewhere!*

She began to visualize tourist-office posters of exotic
lands, making them come to life in her mind and planting
herself squarely in the midst of them. But in each image,
the blue eyes of Tor Christiansen intruded and blurred the
scenic backgrounds. She heard his deep voice provoking
her to anger, washing away the sounds of surf on distant
isles. Her body remembered his towering over her. The
sensation returned—that peculiarly pleasant weakness she
felt when he was near. Carol stopped her fantasizing about
both far-away places and Tor; both were beyond the realm
of her reality . . . a waste of time. It would be far better to
look around at what existed, at the reality of the moment.

The scenery cooperated in a spectacular fashion. She
came out of a steeply graded curve to encounter a view
that took her breath away. Carol pulled the car off to the
side of the road and turned off the engine. She was at a
high point, midway between Oslo and Honefoss. The land
fell away from her on every side. The twisting road that she
had traveled dropped and curled down on her left, and
the road she would travel cascaded down the western side
of the mountain, swirling and bending into a green valley.

The midnight sun lit the panorama. It reached out to

illuminate and soften everything below her. The wild flowers massed in the fields and tumbled down the side of the mountain—heather, buttercups, and bluebells—the colors bright in the northern sun, lush against the silver rocks. She could have stayed on her mountaintop for hours, drinking in the grandeur spread below her. But thoughts of an impatient Tor caused her to start the car and move it back onto the road and down the western slope.

For almost two hours Carol wound and spiraled, threaded and twined her way deeper in the stately Jotenheims. The air grew thinner and the wild flowers sometimes grew up from mounds of snow, undaunted by the white covering. Portions of the slender road were still banked with winter snow, and the close-lying glacier had refused to submit to summer. It was not a leisurely drive, although Carol's eyes took in every view, for the road grew narrower. Approaching cars would often have to back off in order to allow her to pass, and she would do the same for others. She felt the tension building in her shoulders and neck and stopped at the next lay-by to relax for a minute.

She poured a steaming cup of coffee from the thermos and unfolded her map. Carol was appalled that she had come such a short distance, so she gulped the piping hot liquid, mentally apologizing to Inga for not savoring it.

She reached for the ignition. A cloud passed fleetingly overhead and shadowed her hand. Her eyes swept the horizon, her hand suspended over the key. She stared at the majestic scene before her and thought of giants passing by, of angry gods carving out the mountains—and she thought of Tor. She gazed at the huge boulders balanced on the slopes and thought of titans hurling them about in some ancient war of the gods. She imagined a dreamlike, mythical scene—the faces of the giants were clear in her mind, and they all had the startling cobalt eyes of Tor Christiansen. What was happening to her that every simple shadow startled her into fantasies? Carol shook the images from her mind, started the car and moved it back onto the road.

She resolved to make better time; she must not be late for the breakfast meeting. Up ahead, beyond the furthest mountain, a bank of black clouds darkened the glacier on a distant peak. The narrow road, with its steep grades and contracting curves almost turning back in on themselves, would not allow her to travel any faster. She crept along, hugging the wall of rock around each spiral, looking up now and then at the darkening cloud above the mountain. It turned into a thunderhead, the billowing dark masses swirling and piling silently higher and higher. The land of the midnight sun became as black as a London winter, and a few rain drops splashed on the windows.

Carol slowed down near a village called Gol. *I really should stop, I suppose.* But the mocking face of Tor, his eyes challenging her, made her press the accelerator down firmly. After all, it was only rain. And the car was heavy, safe. She turned on the heater to take the chill off, and the warmth immediately blew over her body and calmed her. She would make it to Geilo in time and hand the folder over to the man. She imagined his arrogance changing to astonishment, or at least grudging admiration, and smiled to herself. Her hands tightened firmly on the steering wheel.

Then the mountain storm came down with a vengeance. Carol had never seen such driving rain, such blinding lightning, nor heard such terrifying thunder. The rain came down in sheets, flinging great washes of water against the windshield so that the road disappeared in front of her for frightening moments. Then a great bolt of lightning flashed and the mountains and valleys lit up before her only to disappear into blackness.

She was afraid to go on, and more afraid to stop. She had a vision of the water gushing off the slopes onto the

road and washing her and the car into an unknown abyss
There was no place to pull off, no shelter, not even a wide
place in the road. If she could just get through the storm
just hold the car on the road a little longer.

Perhaps the old Viking gods are angry, she thought, *but
why are they angry at me?* She concentrated on the road
but thoughts of mountain mysteries shot through her
mind as vividly as the lightning searing the black sky. It was
no wonder the old Norse myths grew in these mountains
for the enormity of the storm seemed beyond the realm o
nature, certainly the quiet nature of England. The gods
threw down another titanic fork of screaming light and
roared in fury, the sound echoing from the bowels of the
mountain. Carol focused her mind on reality—the road
the lighted dials on the dashboard, the steady warmth o
the car heater.

Suddenly the right front wheel hit something hard and
solid. The steering wheel spun wildly from Carol's grasp
and the car wrenched into the wall of rock to the right
then out of control to the left, to the side of the road that
Carol knew must cut deeply into a gorge. She screamed in
that one instant of terror as she envisioned the impending
fall and crash. But the heavy body of the car skidded just
off the road, lumbered heavily downward a few feet, and
rolled gently over on its side, wedging itself against a tree
From some hidden reserve of reason, Carol turned off the
ignition, and the engine shuddered thankfully to a stop.

She was lying on her side, leaning heavily against the le
door and held against the seat by her safety belt. She
looked down and through the window she lay against a
the valley sheering off just a few feet from the tree tha
held the car. The thunder rolled around her, and she
began to shake. She was frightened, truly frightened. She
began to tremble uncontrollably, giving way to shock
Finally she was able to take a deep breath and begin t
think again.

She blessed the tree and its strong roots that clung so tightly into the rock. After a few moments, her shoulder began to hurt, but it didn't seem to be more than bruised. She was all in one piece, certainly a miracle. Perhaps the Norse gods had some pity on her. She unfastened the safety belt and tried to climb up the nearly perpendicular seat. By bracing herself against the driver's seat, she was able to reach and push against the right door. But the first crash against the rocks had jammed it tight. She was trapped.

She moved back down the seat, still shaking. The great bulk of the car, which had seemed so vast to her before, now was cramped and claustrophobic. She stared out the cracked windshield, helpless. Outside her prison, the storm began to ease as suddenly as it had begun. The clouds broke into black masses, then thinned to gray wisps against the bright sky. The wind still bent the tops of the trees, and she felt the tree that held the car shift sickeningly.

The new threat, instead of increasing her fear, irrationally made her angry—angry at herself. She should have stopped. The rain was so heavy, the road so narrow. Why did she keep going? What possessed her to continue? And then the most difficult question of all came into her mind. *If I get out of here, what will I say to Tor Christiansen?*

She shifted in her angled seat and felt the thermos bottle, which seemed to be intact, under her feet. Awkwardly, she reached down and got it, then opened it and managed to pour some of the still steaming liquid into her body, now thoroughly chilled in the cold mountain air. She also found one of Inga's cinnamon cookies and chewed it slowly, remembering her bravado in the kitchen a few hours before. She didn't feel at all daring or adventurous now—her impulse had landed her here: cramped, trapped and nearly upside down. She felt both foolish and sorry for herself. But the cookie comforted her, and she vowed, if she ever saw Inga again, that the kind woman would know about it.

Then she heard a car in the distance. Would they see her? Would they stop? Perhaps if she could open the right window, and then wave or shout. She stood on the edge of the seat and tried to roll the window open. It was jammed. The sound of the car was closer . . . a powerful engine, perhaps a sports car. *They won't know I'm here! I'm in a gully, below eye level!* The realization that she had to do something, anything, to stop the oncoming car mobilized her. "Do something now!" she shouted aloud. She reached down and grabbed the thermos, and shielding her face with her sweater, swung the heavy canister against the glass. The window shattered. She hurriedly pulled the shards from the frame and waved her sweater out of the window, shouting as loud as she could. She was above the height of the road . . . if the car wasn't going too fast, they might see her.

She saw the car come around a curve about a hundred meters away, approaching from the west at a great speed. It was a small car, dark colored . . . an MG. Tor! A series of rushing, conflicting emotions streamed through her— relief, shame, and a thrill she found very inappropriate. She almost pulled her sweater back into the car, hating the idea of him seeing her in this state, seeing his car smashed, probably ruined forever. But there was a more important matter than the deep shame she felt. It was survival. Again, Carol waved her sweater wildly and shouted. It might not be Tor in the car.

The MG roared toward her and howled past. *He didn't see me!* she agonized. But then she heard the speeding car braking almost immediately, screeching to a halt and then backing up to the wrecked vehicle and Carol's wildly waving sweater. The driver got out and stared down at her. It was Tor; her dread was realized.

Carol looked up into his face. What she saw was more

than the anger she had dreaded—almost a tortured fury. He stood glaring at her for a moment, his eyes flashing. Finally his voice came, strained and furious, but the words were the right ones. "Are you hurt?"

"No, I don't think so . . . a little bruised, perhaps. Tor, I'm so sorry about the car. The storm came up so . . ."

"Let's get you out of there."

He reached down to grab her under the arms and pulled her through the window frame, lifting her gently and seemingly without effort. Carol didn't weigh much, but Tor lifted her out of the car as though she were a doll. He stood her up on her feet, safe on the roadway, and her legs crumpled beneath her. She was suddenly numb and faint.

Carol felt herself hoisted up, weightless in his arms, and held tight, very close to his body. He carried her to his car, not hurting her, though she felt crushed against his chest, his strong arms cradling her back and thighs. Tor thrust her into the passenger seat and slammed the door. Her head fell limply back. She was conscious but still weak from both shock and relief. Tor went back to the BMW for her grip and the file. He threw them behind his seat and swung his body in beside her. She felt his hands buckling the seat belt across her body. The sound of his voice came to her as though from across a distant valley. "You can smash windows, but cannot find the strength to fasten a seat belt."

She dimly heard the engine roar to life, and she felt the surge of power thrusting her spine against her seat. The machine moved smoothly onto the road, turned around, and headed west, Tor gearing the engine effortlessly up to speed. Carol stared out the window with half-closed eyes, watching the scenery fly by at a terrifying speed. The car seemed to devour the road as Tor raced it around the hairpin curves, accelerating madly up to what appeared to be a drop-off, then going even faster as he turned into the curve, forcing the road to do the car's bidding. Carol almost stopped breathing, her eyes wide open now, her mouth agape. But the ride was smooth, with no wrenching from side to side, no lurching forward in the wrong gear. Without question, Tor knew the road and the car. *If I weren't still shaking inside, I'd be enjoying this ride,* Carol thought. She looked at Tor. *But he doesn't look as if he is. Why should he? His car is wrecked on the side of a mountain, his weekend is ruined because he's had to rescue an incompetent, foolish little English waif . . .*

Carol said, to stop herself from thinking, "How did you find me?"

"I called the apartment and talked to Inga. She is very upset. I don't like that you upset Inga."

"I'm truly sorry, but I think you're angry because I've upset you, not Inga. I just felt it was necessary to get the file to you as soon as possible. Rhys was not . . . feeling well, and so . . ."

"Rhys was either missing or drunk or both, as usual. You will not make excuses for him."

"I wasn't excusing him. But he is your brother. I would be rude to say anything that might . . ."

"Rhys is a liar and a drunk. There is no polite way to say it. He has not done a day's work in his life. He does nothing but smile and chase women, and lie and drink himself sick!"

"Perhaps he's very unhappy. There must be a reason that he hurts so much."

"Do not waste your time trying to understand Rhys. He is lazy and good for nothing. If it were not for my mother and Lisle, I would disown him tomorrow."

There didn't seem to be a reply to that definitive opinion. Obviously Tor hated his brother. *Why?* Carol wondered. *I couldn't hate Rhys for being lazy or drunk. I might be discouraged or impatient with him, but you have to take relatives as they come.* But there was something else in the relationship between the brothers that was hidden from her. *And none of my business,* she told herself firmly.

It was a thought that would not go away. She looked at Tor now, the strong brow furrowed, the eyes intent on the road ahead, the jaw thrust forward, tense and angry. The raw power of the man driving his machine, feeling so much, pulled her into his passions like iron to a human magnet. She forced her mind back to practical matters, drawing a curtain between her mind and her heart.

"I will pay for the damage to your car, of course. It will take me some time . . . I don't make a great deal of money, but I promise that you'll be paid in full."

"That car was custom-made especially for me. It was unique, one of a kind. Months went into the design of special features in the engine. There is no way to calculate its value."

Carol's resolve crumbled. "But . . . I'll do anything I can. I know I should have pulled off the road, but the storm came up so suddenly, and there must have been a fallen rock in the road, and I didn't see . . " Her voice broke and the tears came rushing out.

"Do not cry!" he shouted.

The sound of his voice frightened her and stopped her tears, its fury a wall against her tormenting guilt. Then her torment turned to fury at his insensitivity.

"Don't you shout at me! I feel badly enough without being screamed at by an insensitive ogre!" She was surprised at the vehemence in her voice. From anguish to anger in the space of a few seconds—what was happening to her?

Tor was silent for a moment, and then he said in a more controlled tone, "You are correct. I am sorry, I have no need to shout. You have had a shock, and perhaps you are

77

injured more than you know. We are going to the doctor in Geilo."

"I don't need a doctor. I'm fine."

"Your shoulder pains you, and you're full of scratches. You will see the doctor."

Carol could see that there was no arguing with him. And he was right, of course.

"As to the car, I will have it towed. Perhaps all is not lost. We both judge too quickly."

Carol was mollified by the reason in his voice, but she still fumed inwardly. He could have listened to her explanation of the suddenness of the storm, the difficulty in finding a place to stop — all of the exceptional circumstances that surround accidents. She wasn't giving excuses for what was clearly her fault, but he could have listened. Carol wanted him to listen, wanted him to understand.

They did not speak for the rest of the drive to Geilo. Tor drove up to a quaint chalet and parked. "This is the clinic. The doctor is not busy now. His season is in winter when the tourist skiers break their bones hourly."

The doctor was easily persuaded out of his hip boots, donned for early-morning trout fishing, to examine Carol. He prodded and twisted her gently and thoroughly, daubed antiseptic on her scratches, pronounced her fit and was back into his boots in half an hour.

When Carol left the clinic, Tor was waiting impatiently beside his MG. His tall frame leaning against the low-slung automobile made it look like an elegant toy.

"You are all right, then?"

"Yes, but ..."

Without waiting for more, he slid into the driver's seat. Carol got into the car, feeling a twinge of stiffness in the small of her back. The doctor had told her to expect some stiffness in her muscles, some soreness from the jolt her body had received. She was to rest, keep warm, take hot baths.

"Is there a hotel? I really need some rest, and I ..."

"There are dozens of hotels. But we have no time. I must work with the weld stress file now, this morning. And you must be with me to decipher the Ballinger hieroglyphics. I have supplies at my loft. We will work there."

Oh no, thought Carol, *I can't work. I can't even think about work! My eyes won't stay open.* She couldn't understand why they must go to this "loft." Didn't Rhys say that the mountain cabin was a secret, that no one was allowed to go there? She supposed it didn't matter whether or not she, an incompetent little foreigner, glimpsed the hideaway, since she would be out of the country and his life in a short time.

Tor did not speak as they drove north on a twisting gravel road. Carol trusted his driving completely now. Even if she hadn't, she wouldn't have been able to keep her eyes open. She slept.

About thirty minutes later, she awoke when the sound of the engine stopped. She opened her eyes and saw spread out before her a meadow full of yellow wild flowers dancing in the morning sun against a cyclorama of tall pines. They were in a small valley, the land rolling up to the mountains like a smooth green sea.

Tor was out of the car and striding away, the file and her grip under his arm. She got stiffly out of the car and stood up, following him. The loft house stood on a small rise, a log house that seemed carved out of the wooded land around it. It was rough, rustic, hewn ages ago by some ancient Norseman. The lower level was smaller than the top one—one large square set on top of a smaller one. At the corners, bracing the upper level, were carved pillars and horizontal beams piled on each other in an arching form, giving the structure the same feeling as the Viking ships. The lines were different, of course — the square lines of the house were not the graceful curves of the ships — but the arches, the strength of them and the jutting upper level, gave Carol the sense of a great square ship sailing in the sea of yellow flowers. And on top of the steeply pitched roof, the Viking sea serpent perched menacingly.

Tor stood in the doorway looking back at her. "Well, come along!"

Carol gritted her teeth. Couldn't the man give her a little time to take it all in? She was tired and sore, she had driven through a terrible storm to do him a service, she had been in an accident. Still he stood there glaring at her, impatient and clearly annoyed.

She walked to the loft very slowly, deliberately taking her own good time, even pausing to bend down and touch a flower. She felt his eyes on her. *Why do I feel this need to annoy him?* Carol grew impatient with herself and what she knew was a rather childish display of independence, and hurried toward him. As she approached, he threw open the door and strode in before her. She glanced up at the heavy beamed frame and read "1752" carved roughly into it. She passed through it and entered a dark and cool, windowless room.

She stood still in the darkness, sensing the special nature of the ancient house, the feeling that whatever happened in it, the house itself would endure.

A match flashed in the middle of the room, lighting Tor's face. He lit an oil lamp on a massive wooden table, and the soft glow spread as he trimmed the wick, silhouetting his muscular frame and strong features and casting his shadow on the rough-hewn timbers of the walls. He picked up the lamp. "Come."

She followed him up a narrow stairway. The upper level was one square room with a window in each wall and an open fireplace in the center, coals still alive in it. The room was the same rough timber, the walls and floors worn with a smooth patina from centuries of scrubbing. The starkness was broken by thick wool rugs in bold colors, scattered on the immaculate floor. A huge corner cabinet, intricately carved and decorated, held china and a dozen painted tin canisters. Several large chairs, a bench, and mounds of pillows encircled the fireplace, inviting the visitor to relax in its glow. One generous bed, built into its own alcove, held a heavy quilt, vivid with hand-made designs. Carol's eyes held on the bed, the one bed.

Tor knelt at the fireplace and placed fresh logs on the fire. The flames leaped to his ministrations, and Carol felt welcome warmth.

"It's hard to believe this house is over two hundred and fifty years old," she said conversationally and perched on a wooden chair.

"It has been restored, but the basic structure is original. And there is evidence that it is even older than the date carved above the door."

"Something about it, when we were outside, reminded me of a ship."

"It is so. The first builders of Scandinavia were builders of ships ... the ships always came first. Everything the Norsemen built afterward was as the ships—houses, even furniture." The firelight played on his face and colored his hair red and dancing gold. "All the same principles of nautical engineering, the stress, the supports ..." Carol heard the vibrant energy in his voice, the enthusiasm. "For instance, the corner beams outside ..." He stopped. "But of this you know nothing. It cannot interest you." His voice lost its warmth and he turned away from the fire.

Carol wanted him to continue. It was true that she might not understand stress factors, but she clearly understood the light that came into his eyes and the life into his voice when he spoke of ships. That one moment of human enthusiasm enchanted her, and she remembered the cat Hoppetussa curling around his shoulder, the smile he had given Inga in her kitchen, his careful lecture on aquavit.

"You are ready to work now, ya?" His look dared her to refuse.

Carol braced herself against the fatigue enveloping her body and smiled her best business-like smile. "Yes, of course." She rose and crossed to the broad trestle table where the file lay next to the Ballinger briefcase. She opened it and looked down at the scrawled figures on the first page. They blurred in front of her eyes. Her legs were weak under her. She knew if she didn't lie down immediately, she would crumple to the floor and be asleep before her head touched it.

She closed the file and turned to Tor. "No, I am not ready. I must rest. You'll have to do without me for a while." She looked around the room for a place to lie down, other than the bed, that article being so definitively Tor's.

"Very well. If you must."

"I must. Just for a few minutes. Where ..."

"There is only one bed."

"Thank you." Carol walked over to the bed, sat down on it—or rather in it, the feathers almost enveloping her small frame. She wanted to remove her outer clothes at least, and looked at Tor. He glared at her. Finally he turned away and began to page through the file, allowing her the privacy of his averted eyes. She shed her rumpled slacks and blouse and slipped under the downy warmth of the quilt.

She fell quickly into a twilight sleep—part of her aware of Tor in the room as he moved from studying the files on the table to putting wood on the fire, the other part of her in a darker, deeper place of roaring, storming seas and flashing colors.

She dreamed of Viking ships, their prows slashing through angry waves, taming the turmoil of violent currents. And the giant of the mountain was there, manning the ships, bare-armed with studded bracelets circling enormous biceps, fur skins covering his broad chest. Flowing curls whipped in the sea wind, escaping from a great horned helmet. It was a violent dream, one so close to consciousness that she knew she was dreaming as the visions swirled in her mind. She felt herself on the ship, being lifted by the giant waves and crashing down into the deep watery hollows. And at the same time, she knew she was twisting and turning in the bed. In her dream, the giant watched her cling to the ship, his eyes evil, his broad naked legs spread wide against the deck, his arms folded arrogantly across his chest. The blue eyes challenged her to let go, to stand beside him, dared her to try the tempest with him. Mesmerized by the challenge in his eyes, she let go of the side of the ship. Immediately she was hurled up and forward, thrown into the outstretched arms of the Viking giant. Carol felt her body wrench itself painfully, and she awoke with a start. Tor Christiansen was looking down at her.

But this was no Viking giant, and the eyes held no evil glare. They seemed merely puzzled.

Chapter Six

"YOU HAVE A bad dream?" Tor's voice was gentle.

"I . . . yes, a very bad dream. Did I cry out?"

"Ya, a little . . . little sounds, and breathing very hard."

"Strange. I don't dream at all, usually. But I feel so much better now. It's surprising what just a few minutes can do. I'm quite ready to work now, if I can just freshen up a bit. . ."

"A few minutes? You have slept four hours."

Carol shook her head, disoriented in time and place by her dream and the reality she woke to. She felt the dream disappearing and wanted to hold it, the terrible dream, hold on to its excitement, adventure . . .

"The facilities here are primitive, but you will perhaps be able to adjust to them. Come with me."

He threw her a heavy, deep green robe and started down the stairs. Carol reluctantly crawled out of the comfort of the bed. She put the robe on and was enveloped by the great size and soft warmth of it. She crossed the room and started down the stairway after Tor, feeling the bruises and stiffness in her muscles. The memory of the accident came back to her acutely with the soreness.

In one corner of the lower room there was a small door fashioned of the same rough wood but newer than the rest of the room. Tor opened it to reveal a fully equipped bathroom. "A necessary luxury," he said. He opened another even smaller door inside the bathroom. "Here *badstu*. It will ease your body. Spend some time here after your bath."

Carol looked into the smaller room. "A sauna! So that's what a *badstu* is!"

Tor made a face. " 'Sauna' is a Finnish word. We do not use Finnish words in Norway."

Carol suddenly saw Rhys in Tor's face — the playful mimic Rhys. She dared to play along. "I'm sorry, I thought that 'sauna' was Swedish."

"Oof da! Even worse!"

"I'm sorry. I promise to stay on the correct side of the verbal border from now on."

"Good, then."

Tor put out his hand to shake hers and seal the pact. Her hand felt small inside his. He did not let go until Carol gently pulled away.

"I won't stay long in your sau—*badstu!* I didn't mean to sleep so long ..."

"The mind cannot work if the body is tired or in pain. You and I will work fast when you are refreshed."

He opened a cabinet to show her a great stack of large, soft towels, then left her alone, closing the door behind him.

Carol stared at the closed door and wondered what had happened to the angry man who had driven her there a few hours before? What mountain magic had cast a spell and changed the beast into a gentleman—a very pleasant gentleman? No doubt it was his loft, some time here, away from business pressures. It was another side to Tor, and Carol liked it very much.

Carol soaked in the tub, washed her hair, then dutifully entered the *badstu* and stretched out on the slatted wooden bench, covering her nakedness with one of the large towels. The scented air entered her lungs and she drank deeply of it. The dry heat penetrated the aching muscles and drew the tension out. It felt wonderful. *Another virgin adventure,* she thought, and she threw the towel to the floor, letting the heat touch every seeking surface of her body.

She almost fell asleep again, but some residual sense of duty roused her. She wrapped herself in Tor's big green robe and went back upstairs.

He was waiting for her, but there was no sign of impatience on his face. She saw and felt his eyes travel the length of her, appraising, and she drew the robe tight around herself.

"It's a bit big for me. I must look very silly."

Tor didn't respond. He rose from the table slowly and came very close to her. He looked at her face with a kind of wonder, of discovery, as though he had never seen her before. He reached out and touched her cheek with the back of his hand, tracing the curve of her jaw and throat, exploring its soft, fresh cleanness. He gently fingered her damp curls. "Not silly . . . a sea maid, coming up from the deep water, from the kingdom of the ocean gods, a tiny princess of the sea."

Carol could not move. For one terrifying, wonderful moment, all she knew was the nearness of the man. The touch of his hand, his fresh, sweet smell, the soft words uttered from some secret depth of his own feelings, his own myths, overpowered her. She felt no embarrassment, no shyness. She had no questions. She was open to him, held by a new light in his eyes, a small sun in the Northern ice-blue depths.

Suddenly the light went out and he turned away from her abruptly. Her heart cried out, *Oh, don't turn away! Please stay with me. . . don't. . .* But the moment was gone.

She broke the silence tentatively, watching him bend over the table, shuffling papers. "I know nothing about mermaids . . . your sea maids, but if this is the way they feel, I should very much like to be one."

He shook his head. "They were demons. They tempted the sailors from their ships, luring them to watery deaths. One must constantly be on guard." His voice was flat, unreadable. He pointed to the table where he had laid out a feast of Inga's making. "You will eat something now."

Even the steaming cup of coffee did not tempt her. He was so cold so suddenly. Carol felt her frustration rise. She sat down at the table and nibbled at a sandwich. As she watched the steam rise from her cup she was suddenly washed with a great wave of loneliness and isolation. She had a terrible craving for a cup of tea. It seemed ages since she had left England. Could it really have been less than three days?

"When you are finished, I have questions." The impatience was back in his voice.

Carol rose immediately. "I'm finished now, thank you, and ready to work." She crossed to his chair where he had a file open on his knees. He handed her a page from it.

"Translate, please."

The scrawl on the side of the diagram was embellished with loops, numerals and arrows. Carol studied the scrawl for a moment and then read aloud, "Addition of two more pontoon columns will provide sufficient strength to resist a list of forty-five degrees in any direction, allowing current speeds up to forty knots and seas of fifty feet." Carol paused at the next line.

Tor's voice commanded, "Go on."

She obeyed, trying to keep the amusement from her voice. "Pick up laundry before Tuesday."

Tor paused and frowned. His eyes narrowed to slits, and he said with great deliberation, "Tuesday? You're sure it says Tuesday?"

She answered in the same serious tone, "All the data indicates that Tuesday is the ultimate deadline for laundry." And then the giggle escaped her lips.

Tor's face broke into a grin. He had the most beautiful smile she had ever seen. It changed his stern face into a joyous one, the laughter crinkling around his eyes and mouth. A rumble of laughter joined her giggle. He rose and took the paper from her and put it back into the file, then slapped the file back on the table.

"It is no good to work here. It never is, in my harbor.

That is what I call this place—my 'harbor.' We will work tomorrow in Bergen. Today, we rest and play! Get dressed. We go to Geilo. They have their Midsummer Festival. You will enjoy it." He gathered the files into his briefcase and added, "Bring your luggage. We'll leave for Bergen after a late lunch." He went down the stairs to allow her to dress in private.

Rhys had said that Tor never played, yet here he had announced his intention to do just that, to spend some time with her—playing.

She dressed quickly in the new, bright blue skirt and white sweater. She ran a brush through her now dry hair and didn't even consider pinning it back. It bounced on her shoulders in hopeless disarray as she grabbed her suitcase and skipped down the stairs and out into the early afternoon sun. Tor was waiting at the car. His eyes moved over her swiftly, and although he said nothing, she felt he approved. A small, warm spot of happiness grew in her. *I can read his eyes,* she thought. *I'm beginning to know him.* And that knowledge made her very happy.

Carol recognized the road. They had traveled it that very morning on the way from Geilo to the loft. But it was a different world. The sun shone brightly on the mountains, which now seemed gentle and worn rather than the threatening monsters that had so terrified her the night before. The huge boulders rested securely, serenely, and many little loft houses nestled in the hollows of the hills. The sharp clean air was a tonic, and Carol felt infused with vigor and life. Certainly the man beside her was part of that different world. Gone was the anger, the menace, even the condescending tone in his voice.

"You know of midsummer?"

"No, is it a special holiday in Geilo?"

"It is a special holiday everywhere in Norway. You would know how special it is if you had ever spent a winter here with day and night wrapped in darkness."

Carol thought of the London winter, both time and place very far away at this moment. "At home, it is so gray for so many months. I know times when I have absolutely craved a glimpse of the sun."

He smiled as he glanced sideways at her. "I remember the London grayness, but it is not so dark as our winter. The coming of light is very special to us, and we celebrate. Today is the day of all festivals, the longest day. Tonight, on every mountain top, the bonfires will be lit by the families who live there. And everyone will dance."

The village of Geilo was a carnival of color. Food stands displayed a variety of tempting delicacies. Craftsmen proudly spread out their wares—beautiful hand-knit sweaters, scarves and mittens, intricate models of ships with sails fluttering in the mountain wind, jewelry of hammered gold and silver and pewter, glazed pottery in colors of depth and richness—an entire spectrum of bold colors in each piece. Groups of musicians tuned their instruments and played lively tunes. And children dressed in native costumes gathered in groups to sing and dance, performing for proud parents and smiling tourists.

Carol and Tor ate thick molasses cookies as they strolled among the booths. "I can't decide what to buy," wailed Carol. "I want three of everything, and I'll never get them in my suitcase!"

When they came to a booth of wood carvings, Carol grabbed Tor by the arm and propelled him closer. Tor protested, laughing, "So much muscle for such a little person! You will tear my arm from the socket!"

"But look, Tor! What are they?"

"Trolls—you must have one to remember Norway."

Carol exclaimed over each figure, each intricately carved little gnome, coveting each one.

"Look, Tor! This one looks like Mr. McKinzie! His hair stands up just like that!"

"You must beware of him then. All trolls are angry and

very vicious. He'll kidnap you and carry you to his cave in the mountains. You'll never be seen again!"

"And this lady troll with the red nose. She looks like my landlady in London. She glares at me just like that every time I pass her door! Oh, look! What are these little tiny trolls?"

"Those are not trolls. They are nissen. Nissen are good luck—mischievous but good. One can never see a nisson, except from the corner of the eye. They hide and peek around things at us, deciding whether to be good or to sour the milk."

"I must have one of those too!"

Carol knew she must have her very own troll and nisson, but she couldn't make a decision. Finally Tor threw up his hands in mock horror. "This is impossible! We will be among trolls until next midsummer! Close your eyes and do not open until I say so! I will chose."

Carol obeyed, thinking that the selection of a troll was in good hands. Hadn't Rhys called Tor the "Head Troll?" She started to giggle.

"Shush!" Tor said sternly. "I make a major executive decision and cannot have laughter."

There were rapid words between Tor and the woodcarver and much shuffling about. Finally, Tor said, "All right—open your eyes and see!"

He held out a mesh shopping bag that was stuffed full of trolls — large and small, twinkling, menacing, squat and skinny. Through the mesh poked red noses and fat bellies, tiny feet both bare and booted, ogling eyes and evil grins. Clambering around the trolls were the nissen, peeking over troll shoulders and between troll ears. Tor deposited the ungainly bag in her arms and said, "Now you have one for every mood, every occasion, and also a bag full of luck."

Carol protested to no avail, then laughed and accepted it all. She groped for words she had heard from Inga and remembered. *"Tusen, tusen takk,* many thanks!" And she smiled into his eyes her pleasure.

Tor's eyes laughed with her for a moment, then suddenly grew serious and wondering, the light in their blueness washing over her with a warmth she could feel deep inside her body. The time was so intense that Carol did not know if it was an instant or an eternity. Finally, she looked down shyly, confused. Tor shook her hand gently, and they started toward a chalet that was nestled in the mountain-side.

She knew she would treasure this moment, however brief—the clear mountain air and shining light, the sense of freedom, the warmth of the big strong hand holding hers.

Suddenly she looked down and saw the Mr. McKinzie troll falling through the mesh of the bag, its head almost touching the grass. "They're escaping!" she shouted. "Quick, help me!"

Tor went into action. "It is very bad to let them escape!" Both struggled to push the heads and noses and little gnome bodies into the bag, laughing and shrieking like children. They would push a troll back in, and a nisson would pop out. They'd catch the nisson, and a troll would wiggle out. Finally Tor peeled off his sweater. "Wrap them up in this, or they will run to the mountains and throw boulders down on us!" They wrapped the figures in his sweater, and Tor gathered it up and placed the bundle securely in her arms. He stood back and looked at her as she cradled the soft bundle.

"When we go in to lunch, if anyone asks to see the baby, tell them he's got the croup!" This sent them into a new gale of laughter that brought them to the door of the chalet.

They controlled their wonderfully foolish laughter and went their separate ways to wash. When Carol returned, she saw Tor talking with a group of men, clearly old friends of his. Carol decided not to disturb them. She wandered into the lounge, a cozy sunken room with an enormous fireplace. Oversize sofas surrounded the wide hearth and great pillows were scattered invitingly around the floor. Carol imagined the scene in winter, skiers draping themselves over the pillows, sprawled and glowing with hot mulled wine, telling stories of the slopes.

Near the entry were a great many photographs of skiers against the glaring white of the winter snow, some in action, some groups posed smiling and red-cheeked, beautifully sweatered and jacketed. Then she saw a picture of Tor, standing tall against the mountain. And next to him, nearly as tall, a dark, laughing girl. Their arms were holding each other—the easy, familiar way of lovers. The next picture was a closer shot, the girl laughing into the camera, Tor looking at her with adoration in his eyes.

I can never compete with that, not even if I wanted to. That must be Joleen, the American girl. She looks American, free and brash and unafraid of anything. Tor might amuse himself with me for an afternoon, Carol thought, *but he truly loved that girl.* She was sad for both of them, said that their love had died with Joleen. And she felt distant from Tor and despaired of ever having anything like that love for herself.

Tor was looking for her when she entered the dining room. They sat at a table that commanded a view of flowered meadow and towering mountain and ordered wine with their fresh-caught trout.

"You are very quiet," observed Tor as they savored their coffee.

"It's been a very eventful day. I think it's all just catching up with me."

"You are tired?"

"No, not at all! I was just thinking about . . ." There was no point in telling him the truth, telling him that her thoughts had been of him and Joleen, of the times they must have spent in this very chalet. She detoured to an obvious topic. "I was thinking about your poor car, and how I'll never be able to make it up to you."

"The car doesn't matter. It wasn't entirely your fault. If Rhys had done as he should have ..."

"But I feel responsible. And you were so angry."

"Angry?" He seemed genuinely puzzled.

"Of course you were! When you came at me out there on the road, I thought you were going to push me and the car the rest of the way down the gorge! And I wouldn't have blamed you if you had."

A look of confusion came over Tor's face. He put his head in his hands and stared down at the table, his breathing heavy, labored.

"Tor, are you ill? Did I say something? What's wrong?"

"Nothing," he rasped and looked up at her. "I am not ill and I was not angry. Let's say no more about it. Come, it's time to go." He stood up and headed for the door.

In the car Tor's jaw was set and silent. Carol dared not speak, even to casually comment on the scenery. The tension in him seemed to vibrate in the confines of the sports car, and Carol felt the echoes of his anger inside her own body. For it had to be anger, regardless of his denial. She had thought it was over, ever since she awoke that morning and found him so kind, even solicitous of her well-being. Apparently, she wrong. The child-like joy they had shared for a few hours faded into the past.

They drove into a small service station, where the BMW was ensconced on a lift. Tor got out of the car and went to talk to the mechanic without a word to her. But she wanted to know the worst, so she followed, standing close to hear the verdict.

The two men were deep in serious discussion, but of course it was in Norwegian, and she would have to wait for the translation. She saw Tor nod, and there was an appropriate silence for her question.

"How bad is it, Tor?"

His answer was terse, as though he was annoyed at such a simple question. "The engine is fine, and the frame."

"Then it's just the body that needs work?"

"Yes. I will have it fixed in Bergen. The man here has balanced the wheels and put in a temporary window. It can be driven."

"I'm so glad!" She paused and considered a moment. She had to make the effort to accommodate him as much as possible. "If you'll trust me, I will drive it for you, so you won't have to hire someone to bring it to Bergen."

Tor turned to stare at her. "You dare to drive it again, after what happened last night?"

Carol laughed ruefully. "Of course. You know the saying, that if you fall off a horse, you must get back on directly, or you'll never ride again!"

"Where did you learn that!?" The vehemence with which he asked the question made Carol back up a step.

"What do you mean? It's just an old saying. I've heard it for years. I believe it's a Britishism."

"Americans also say it." This seemed to close the subject. He spoke to the mechanic, who started to lower the BMW from the lift.

Joleen again! Carol's mere existence seemed to remind Tor of the American. Understandably, the memory might be sad, but why should it provoke anger? *Is he angry because I'm alive and she's dead?*

The mechanic drove the car into the sunshine and got out, holding the door for her. Tor said, "You will follow behind me. Flash your lights if you have trouble, or if I am driving too fast. Do not get more than fifty meters behind me." Without another word, he got into his sports car and gunned the engine. Carol got into the BMW, shifted into low gear, and they headed toward Bergen.

At first Carol thought Tor was being especially careful by driving so slowly, but the pace was ridiculous. Perhaps he

94

was punishing her. Or challenging her to pass him? Whatever the reason for the snail's pace, she would not yield to either his punishment or the imagined challenge. She gritted her teeth and kept the car in low gears.

After an hour, Tor began to drive at a more reasonable speed. Perhaps seeing that she hadn't driven into a mountain or a gorge reassured him. They began to make better time, and having him directly ahead gave her confidence. She began to enjoy the drive and the scenery.

Several hours later, Carol felt the nearness of the fjord before she saw it. There was a sense that something monumental was just ahead. She had seen enough tourist brochures to know that the western fjord country was nature at its most awe-inspiring, but their descent to the mighty Hardangerfjord was more spectacular than she could imagine, more than any glossy photograph could begin to capture. She gasped audibly as the vast and wild scene opened before her, striking her sight and sensibility with its untamed grandeur. The descent went all too quickly, too fast for her to take in.

A ferry was about to leave, and Tor was in no mood to dawdle. They drove on and parked the cars, and Tor disappeared. As Carol walked about the boat, he was nowhere to be seen. But when she glanced up at the wheel house, there was Tor, standing next to the captain of the ferry, staring down at her.

She looked away and lectured herself. *You have something far better to do than worry about what he's thinking. Look around you, silly goose, you've never seen anything like this, and probably never will again!*

Carol felt the weariness of the drive fall away from her as she stood at the rail of the ferry, breathing deeply of the clear air and drinking in the beauty of the fjord. Sheer cliffs rose straight out of the water, topped by snow and ice. The mountains beyond guarded the fjord, grand in their majesty, in absolute command of the water below.

Two American children, standing next to her at the rail, couldn't contain their reactions. "Guess what? My mom said you could drop the Empire State Building into this water and it would just disappear. Boy, that's deep! And you know what else? There's a rock called the 'Troll's Tongue,' and it juts way out over the water, and we're going to climb out on it tomorrow! This fjord is a hundred miles long! I bet we'll ride this boat forever and forever!"

Carol was affected by their enthusiasm. She felt like a child too, gazing out and up at the cascading waterfalls, the tiny houses clinging to the mountains, the deep water, the sun shining across the glistening waves on a vast array of boats, keels and sails white in the wind.

She would have forgotten all about Tor Christiansen as she drank in the beauty around her if only she didn't see his eyes staring up at her from the depths of the water, if she didn't see his strong shoulders in the shape of the cliffs, if his smile didn't keep breaking into her vision, outshining the sun.

After a time, Carol sensed she was being watched. Several times she turned to see Tor quite near her. When she tried to speak to him, to offer some comment on the view, he turned abruptly away. But then she would feel his eyes again and turn to find him near. Carol felt part of a strange game, a game in which she didn't know the rules. She resolved to quit the game, to ignore the hovering man. She stared into the water, wondering at its blueness, its depth. She watched the waves created by the ferry boiling up beside the boat and wondered what lay beneath those waves ...

She felt Tor's hand on her shoulder. "Do not hang over like that!" He removed his hand and spoke more quietly. "The sirens sing to everyone, not only the sailors." He gestured toward the cars. "We dock in a few minutes." And he walked away.

Carol touched the shoulder he had held. The conflic

between the warmth of his hand and the coldness of his words confused her. As she made her way back to the BMW, all she could think of was how tired she was of being confused.

After the ferry across the Hardangerfjord, the rest of the drive seemed short in spite of Carol's fatigue. The two cars soon approached Norway's second largest city. Carol had expected the mountains to end and to see Bergen lying flat at the edge of the North Sea. But the mountains did not yield, nor did the ocean. The city of Bergen clung to the conflict between them, proud and tenacious. The lights of the traffic and the city created a river of light that flowed to the sea. Red tile roofs poked up from green parks, and the land jutted into the water which held hundreds, perhaps thousands of boats. Tiny peninsulas fingered into the sea, and the sea reached back to the land, seeking its harbors. The sea and the land—and the people—were joined here in the evening sun, hands entwined. Carol felt, for the first time in her life, actual love for a place.

But the MG ahead of her did not pause, and she followed it without slowing for more reflection. She made a solemn promise to herself. *I will spend time in this place. I don't know how or when, but I will. . . I will*

Chapter Seven

THE CHRISTIANSEN HOUSE in Bergen was on the edge of the city, perched on a hill overlooking the sea. It was a strong, rectangular structure of logs, elegant in its simplicity. The entire facade was punctuated with gleaming windows, and the wild flowers blooming on the hillside echoed the white trim of the house. Carol was aware of the nearness of the sea as she walked behind Tor to the heavy, carved front door. There was a warmth about the house, not only because of the soft brown of the wood, but a certain welcome from the windows and flowers dancing in boxes under each one. This was a home, very different from the machine-like apartment in Oslo.

Tor held the door for Carol, polite, indifferent. The warm feelings she had when seeing his home for the first time disappeared, and she shivered.

They were greeted immediately in the entry by two women, one a little, round, middle-aged lady, red-faced and beaming, who took Carol's grip from her and stood waiting as Carol was presented to the other woman.

"Mor, this is Miss Smythe, from McKinzie in London. She is doing some work for us. Miss Smythe, my mother, Helge Christiansen. And Grete."

Mrs. Christiansen shook her hand firmly and formally, nodding. She turned and spoke rapidly in Norwegian to Tor, who seemed upset at the words and ran up the stairs without a backward glance. He had clearly delegated the duty of attendance on to his mother and the little round lady.

Mrs. Christiansen's eyes traveled the length of Carol before she spoke. "You are welcome to our house. Tor has some business matters to attend to. Grete will see you to your room. You wish to rest from your long drive?"

"Yes, please, if Tor . . . if Mr. Christiansen doesn't need me for a little while."

"Probably not for some time. There is some difficulty on one of the rigs. He must see to it."

Mrs. Christiansen then rattled off some phrases to the still beaming Grete and left the entry briskly. *Well,* thought Carol, *they are certainly mother and son. She's quite handsome and imposing and she didn't smile at me once.*

Grete was entirely the opposite. As soon as the other woman left, Grete began babbling in Norwegian, gesturing for Carol to follow her. With a conspiratorial air, she led Carol on a tour of the main floor. Grete's gestures were broad and a bit theatrical, her voice varied from boom to whisper. The words were unintelligible, but apparently were descriptions of the premises.

All the walls and ceilings were of natural wood, polished to a shine, giving the house a warm, solid quality. Grete paused in her enthusiastic monologue at the door of a large sitting room. "Ya? Ya?" she asked, clearly wanting Carol to approve.

"Oh, yes," breathed Carol, as she took in the inviting space. It was scattered with deep couches, dominated by walls of books and a fireplace with a raised hearth. She returned Grete's enthusiasm in her own language. "I could curl up in this room and never leave, Grete!"

Grete smile widened, understanding Carol's reaction if not the English words. Spurred on, Grete delighted in showing off the spotless kitchen, the large cozy dining room and a rabbit-warren of a space full of ski, skating and fishing equipment. They passed a large polished door that was firmly closed, and Grete put a restraining hand on Carol's arm. "Tor," she whispered in a tone that could only be described as reverent.

Grete and Carol continued the tour, both exclaiming in

their respective languages, understanding each other perfectly. As they mounted the carved wooden stairway, Carol caught the names of Rhys and Lisle and thought, *They have their place here. This is "home" to all of them in the truest sense of the word.* A stab of longing went through her. It had been so many years since she had a home, roots in a place where a real family held her, touched her. *I don't remember what it's like . . . my little flat is where I live, but it isn't home, never will be.*

Grete stood in the doorway of a bedroom, apparently the climax of the tour. She made an entrance to it, placed Carol's suitcase on a chest, gestured dramatically about the room, and exited with a flourish, closing the door behind her.

Carol, alone in the room, turned to look around. "A four-poster!" She walked toward the huge pine bed, taking in the sheer wool curtains that hung around it, ready to be closed to make a luxurious cocoon for the sleeper. She stood in the soft lamplight, looking at the wicker baskets of fresh wild flowers, the carved dresser, the antique cradle in the shape of a Viking ship at the foot of the bed. The deep goose down comforter and pillows were far more interesting than the rest of the furniture, an invitation to rest. Kicking off her shoes, she buried herself in the soft feather quilt. She closed her eyes.

Again it happened—the rush of conflicting emotions piling up inside her, from the welcome she felt at the sight of the house to the anger at Tor to the forbidding reserve of Mrs. Christiansen to the dramatics of Grete to . . . She tried to still them, to still all thoughts of it. She lay in the depths of the feather bed and thought of the placid life she had lived up to a few days before. *I long to return to it,* she thought, *to a time and place where I felt hardly anything at all*! And then she thought, *No, I can't bear to return to it*! She knew both thoughts were absolutely true, and sighed at the conflict. The sigh barely finished before she fell deeply and totally asleep. And this time, she did not dream of anything at all.

Before she was fully awake, she felt the presence of another person very near. Her first dazed thought was that Grete had returned. Then, as she struggled through the mist toward consciousness, she thought of Tor, standing over her as he had in the loft, staring down at her. She opened her eyes in confused panic. But it was neither Grete nor Tor. A young girl, whom she had never seen before, sat on the foot of the bed, her knees drawn up in front of her, chin resting on them, eyes intently on Carol. Carol had no idea how long she had been studied with such scrutiny.

"Please wake! You are asleep for hours. Hello, I'm Lisle." The girl reached over the mound of quilt, grabbed Carol's hand and pumped it firmly once. "We must know each other. Rhys says you are smash! He calls. He comes tonight to Bergen. I am racer. I go for Olympic trials in three days. Do you skate?"

Coming out of a dead sleep, Carol wasn't sure she followed the non-stop words, but she sat up and managed an answer. "You mean, on ice? Er . . . no, actually . . . I never . . ."

"Oh, you ski."

"No, I . . ."

"Then what do you *do?*" Lisle's list of life's activities seemed to consist of only the two items.

Carol shook her hair and some of the cobwebs from her mind and said, "Well, mainly I work for a living, and sleep when I'm not being crossed-examined by total strangers who perch at the foot of my bed."

Lisle laughed at the reproof. "But we are not these strangers. Rhys has tell me all around you! We will be the great friends."

"Even if I don't skate or ski?"

"That is difficulty. Joleen could do everything!"

Joleen had nothing to do with her, and yet each time her name or image appeared, the sensation Carol felt was the same ... a sharp, unpleasant feeling in the pit of her stomach.

"Why should I be able to do what your Joleen could do?"

"My Joleen? No, she was Tor's. But she was much good at everything. And she played with me many lots. That was when I was child, of course. She died horrible in car crash —all smash to pieces. Stupid way. She was terrific driver too. But maybe she wasn't driver, so is all right."

Carol couldn't unravel the logic in Lisle's last statement, and she decided not to try. The girl evidently worshipped Joleen—the do-everything-well, attractive, vital woman that Tor had loved. Carol felt the sharp feeling in her stomach rise in a rush of blood to her face, an anger against the dead woman. Jealousy? Surely not—how irrational! Yet she felt the heat of it, boiling inside her. And she knew that the feeling had been there inside her, seething and building, ever since she had first heard about Joleen. Now it had a name.

She jumped out of bed, hiding the blush in her face and the shock of recognition at her own feelings.

"I fell asleep in my clothes. They're a mess, I'm afraid."

"You look fine. But you can wear some of mine. We're the alike size, if you think so!"

Carol thanked her but refused, anxious to wear her own new clothes. She was pleased at Lisle's openness and generosity. Lisle was indeed about her size. At fourteen or fifteen, she was slim, her slimness all muscular, without a soft place anywhere. She squirmed around on the now empty bed, in no hurry to leave.

"You will to the race on Friday come? Everyone will be there. For years and years I work for this."

"I'd like to, if Tor doesn't have work for me. I must get on with transcribing some important notes."

Lisle slammed her fist into Carol's pillow. "No! He mustn't! And he must be there! Tor must not work on day of race! I will kill him so dead!"

The vehemence took Carol by surprise. "Does Tor usually attend your races?"

"No, he works! All he does is work."

Something made Carol ask, "Does Solveig Folkdahl come?"

"Ha! If Tor is in a place, Solveig is there. But Solveig doesn't care about me or about race. Only Tor. She is very much rich from the fish. She is 'Sardine Queen'!" Lisle grinned. "Rhys and me, we make that up. Is funny in English?"

Carol returned the smile. But she wanted to laugh out loud . . . "Sardine Queen" struck her as very funny, but one didn't comment that strongly on strangers.

Lisle sped on. "English is funny language—like birds' chirps! Tor used to come, when Joleen was alive. They never miss my race. Now he just works and works. He does nothing of fun. Tor skis super! He was contender in jump. Rhys is downhill sometimes slalom!"

"Could Rhys have been a 'contender' also?"

"Ya, he was! He make downhill team the year Joleen was kill. After that, he stop. He was in the car, you see. In the accident with Joleen. But he is not bad hurt. But does not ski no more." With that Lisle bounced off the bed. "I must go to work out with the weights . . . I will see you at supper. Don't let Grete talk your arms and legs off. We are the great friends, ya?" And she went out the door, slamming it after her.

Rhys had been in the car! Could he have been the driver? Had he been drunk? Did Tor hold him responsible for the death of the girl he had loved so much? The questions collided in Carol's brain. Did that violent death change the two brothers? What were they like before?

A feeling of sympathy for Tor's suffering, and for that of

Rhys, came over Carol. To know such tragedy must be a deeply disturbing thing, one that might last for years. Perhaps even Mrs. Christiansen had taken Joleen into the family in the happy hope that there would be strong, healthy grandchildren.

A knock on the door interrupted her melancholic sympathies. It was Grete, who with voluable good will and much gesturing, communicated that Tor waited for her downstairs and that Carol should come down as soon as she was dressed. Grete finished her message with a flourish of arms and a stream of "Ya's" and exited.

Carol bathed quickly, then pulled a soft teal blue jersey over her head and wrapped a toast-colored skirt around her slim waist. As she brushed her hair, she noticed how much softer the waves had become and how they framed her delicate face in a flattering halo. She found herself pleased with her appearance, and wondered if Tor would be too, then quickly pushed the thought out of her mind. He noticed nothing but his work and whatever dark thoughts consumed him. The afternoon in the mountains must have been a momentary aberration. She cancelled her thoughts as romantic self-indulgence and left her room.

As she descended the stairs, Carol put herself into a business-like frame of mind. She took a deep breath and firmly rapped on the door Grete had indicated as that to Tor's room.

"Come."

She went in, imagining some kind of dark cavern but finding instead a lovely, warm room with a corner fireplace, full of books and furnishings of bright, primary colors. The rug was especially handsome—thick white wool with a swirling pattern of blue and beige. Shelves with carvings, ship models and trophies . . . but she was not allowed to indulge in appreciation for details of decor.

"There is much to do. I have begun with the marine

acoustics file. Please go over what I've written, correct it and then we will continue together." Tor's voice was abrupt, the depth and musicality of it blunted with efficiency.

"Of course." Carol's voice was formal in spite of the confusion she felt at the sight of him standing there, dominating his space with casual elegance. His sport shirt of navy cashmere was open at the neck, sleeves rolled part way up his muscular arms. The twill slacks were perfectly cut and fit his lean hips without a crease.

"Sit there, across the desk from me. You see I have made notes next to Ballinger's . . ."

They began to work through the papers one by one, Carol translating the scrawls, Tor comprehending and adding clarifying phrases. They had completed two files when Grete bustled in, laden with a coffee tray, demanding their attention. She arranged giant squares of apple cake, crowned with freshly whipped cream, on the low birch table near the fire. Grete served the coffee as though it were a feast for the Crown Prince. Even Tor smiled after Grete had left. "She takes great pleasure in feeding us. Each serving is a performance. Perhaps she spends too much time at the cinema. But her timing is good, ya? Come and we take the coffee break."

They sat on the sofa. The work had been intense and the break was welcome. But Carol was determined that it would be no more than that, regardless of Tor's pleasantry about Grete. His manner was still formal, and hers would be too.

"Has she been with your family long?" she asked. She wanted to interrupt her own question with an enthusiastic whoop for the taste of the moist apple cake, but she controlled herself.

"Twenty years. Mor could not do without her."

"Has your mother been a widow long?"

"Almost ten years now. My father drowned, an ironic tragedy. He was fishing for pleasure, a few miles off shore.

His whole life was as a fisherman for business, sailing the roughest waters of the North Sea. My mother, she worked alongside him in their young days. Mor is a strong woman in all ways."

Carol had no doubt about that, remembering the serious, impeccably groomed woman who had greeted her so briskly that morning. She couldn't imagine her on a fishing boat, probably dressed in a slicker and big boots, doing hard physical labor, but she supposed it was possible.

"It must be wonderful," Carol mused aloud, "to be able to work with one's husband, side by side, especially against the elements . . . very hard work, I imagine."

"They had a very special relationship, it is true." Tor was already on his second cup of coffee. He relaxed back into the pillows of the sofa. "Mor only took time to have her babies, separated far apart as we are. For her, life was with my father on his boat. After Lisle came, he retired and was content to stay on the land. Only Mor spoke of missing the sea. When he died, she changed. She will not leave the land not go near the boats or the sea she loved. She will not forgive the sea for taking him. Drowning—it is the most horrible way to die for the sailor. All live with the fear of that death."

Tor became silent, staring at nothing. Carol felt the sadness of the man, the love for his family, regret for the love that was lost to his mother. Forgetting her resolve to keep aloof, she impulsively touched his shoulder. He stiffened, and she withdrew her hand, quickly reaching for her coffee cup.

She said, a bit too loudly, "The news from the office your mother spoke of this morning . . . has the problem been solved?"

"No, not solved. The computer indicates one of the rig cables shows signs of instability. It is not dangerous as long as the weather holds. My men are working on the problem." He rose from the sofa. "You have finished your coffee?"

Carol hastened to do so and then crossed to the desk. As she passed a collection of framed photographs on the wall, she paused for a fraction of a second to see a small boy, bundled against the cold, skis in hand, posed in front of a ski jump which towered up and into the background.

Tor was standing near her during that fraction of a second. "My first competition." He reached over her shoulder, his arm brushing her hair, to point to the jump itself. "A thirty meter hill. I was eleven."

"Isn't that awfully young?" Carol felt trapped between the photograph and his towering physical presence behind her. If she moved at all, she would come into full contact with him.

"In Norway, we start jumping very early. I engineered my own hill, behind the house, when I was only six. I almost killed myself on it. It is best to ride hills designed by the experts."

She stared at the photograph, needing a focus for her mind while her body sensed the warmth of his so near her. "I'd love to hear all about it sometime," she said, thinking she would love to hear all about everything involving Tor Christiansen.

His voice was very quiet but she felt his breath against her temple. "It's all ancient history." He turned and walked to the desk, and Carol began to breathe again.

Tor drew his chair around the desk, so they could both examine the papers at the same time, hoping to make the work go faster. They began the next file. Often their hands or arms touched as they pointed out a word or made a note. Carol felt the fleeting warmth of his strong limbs touching hers and the steady heat of his body so close by her side. And there was the smell of the man, the clean, sweet smell she noticed in the loft when he had touched her hair and talked of mermaids. She found breathing growing difficult, and she exerted great effort to keep it even, to keep her voice in control, her mind on the figures in front of her.

Suddenly, his hand closed on top of hers. The size and strength, the warmth of it, stilled both her hand and heart for a moment. She drew a breath and turned her face to his. And she knew the restlessness she was feeling, the growing consciousness of Tor as a man, had grown in Tor toward her as a woman. It was there in the sea of his eyes. Its brightness pierced her like lightning, locking her gaze to his with a current that she felt in every part of her. He bent his face to hers, and she reached for him with aching eagerness. His lips on hers were hungry, searching, demanding. She felt herself respond, her lips parting wanting to give him whatever he desired, whatever he searched for in her, whatever he might demand of her. The force of his mouth on hers, the power of his hands on her shoulders drawing her closer, sent a shudder of weakness and a shock of strength through her. She felt his hands lift her from the chair and his arms fold her close to his body, the length of her pressed tightly against his own. Tidal waves of strength, of weakness, surged through her again and again. She felt her own arms go up around his broad, hard shoulders and then to his neck. The kiss was strong and then gentle—moving, searching, not ending. His hands moved down her back, to encircle and pull her even closer to him. She wanted it to never end.

Suddenly Tor stiffened. She felt his body go rigid along her own a second before he pulled his mouth away from hers. She looked up at him, confused by his withdrawal. It was there in his eyes again—the pain or anger, whatever fire had burned there before when he found her in the wrecked car and leaning over the rail of the ferry. His hands held her shoulders. Carol was afraid. She pulled away and turned from him, the currents crossing and clashing in her brain like the mountain storm. She grasped the back of her chair for a moment, then moved haltingly across the room to the sofa and sat down.

She tried desperately to control the frantic beating of her heart, the tremors in her legs, the rapid breathing. She was finally able to take a deep breath and let it out slowly.

She looked up. Tor stood with his back to her, his hands grasping either edge of the desk, his head down and shoulders bowed over them. It seemed that he would tear the solid surface apart with his hands. The knuckles were white against the wood.

There must be a reason, a logical explanation. Carol searched her mind for one, but she could not explain her own behavior, much less Tor's. What could she do? What could she say? If she could just stop trembling, if she could break this heavy silence . . .

Finally the man turned to her. From across the room his face was impassive, his body erect and still. There was no visible sign of the incredible passion of the moment before. Or had he not felt it? Carol's heart sank with that thought. If it hadn't been real with him, if he had merely played with her, brought her so close to giving herself to him . . . And even if he had felt something, was it no more than the maleness in him coming into life after so many years of diverting it into his work, his moods, his anger? It could be that, only that.

When he spoke, his voice was even. "I'm sorry. She . . . someone used to call me 'Tidal Wave Tor.' It was meant to be funny, but it is not. Perhaps you will be kind enough to type up the material we have covered. We can begin again tomorrow, at my office." He turned and walked out of the room.

Carol did not know how long she sat there. At length she looked around the room, the same cheerful room she had entered a few hours before. Was she the same woman she had been then? Had the fire she felt changed her? Carol shook her head to dismiss such mad thoughts. Of course she was the same. It had been nothing, a mere physical encounter. She would not think about it. She rose and crossed to the desk, seated herself and put paper into the typewriter.

It was agonizing. Every mark Tor had made on the papers recalled the touch of his hand. Every indication of a suggested phrase made his voice sing softly in her mind. But she forced her hands to the keys and began to work. Her logical mind and practiced fingers sorted and arranged the material. But each time she paused, her thoughts went racing back to that moment they were so close; her body reached out to recapture the sensations she had felt; her mind sought out the reasons for his passion, for his abrupt dismissal of it and of her.

How could this be happening? She was more vulnerable than she knew, that was all, and had learned a lesson from it. *Of course I'm attracted to him. He's an attractive man. And that's all there is to it—a momentary attraction. "Tidal Wave Tor" indeed!* Tor Christiansen was probably just releasing long-buried frustrations. Or perhaps he wasn't frustated at all. There was Solveig Folkdahl.

Her fingers flew over the keys, and she finished typing the material in an hour. As she stacked and ordered the pages, she found that much of the material made sense to her. Tor's explanations, comments, and additions to the Ballinger material had clarified it. She would never be an engineer, but a basic understanding of the formulas and terms finally seemed to bear some relationship to the drawings, to the structures and functions they represented. Carol wished her feelings made the same kind of mathematical sense. She covered the typewriter, cleared the desk, and placed her notes neatly in the file. Tor would be pleased.

What do I care whether or not Tor is pleased! She shouted at herself inwardly, scolding and resolving not to think about him or the episode ever again. She knew she lied to herself. She would not forget it for a very long time.

Carol went upstairs and began to draw a bath in the immense tub. It seemed she was constantly leaping in and out of tubs and showers and saunas, but they seemed so special in this country. As she sank into the hot water and scrubbed herself with a vengeance, it was as though she was trying to cleanse her skin of the memory of Tor's hands. But nothing could erase it. She lay back in the tub and let the water caress her, the steam rising around her and easing the muscles of her body if not the turmoil in her mind.

She deliberately chose her most "English" dress—soft lawn green sprigged with tiny flowers. It had a decided Victorian air to it with narrow ruffles at throat and wrists and an inset of tawny lace across the bodice. *Very proper and terribly prim,* she thought as she looked in the mirror.

She brushed the auburn length of her hair with determined strokes, then wrapped the waves tightly to the back of her neck in the twist that had served her so well for so long. But it would not stay bound. The more she tried to control the wisps and waves, the more they escaped to trail down the nape of her neck, to curl resolutely about her ears. It was as if, having tasted freedom, the very hair on her head would never be imprisoned again. She gave up, removed all the pins, ran the brush through it a few cursory times, and rose to go downstairs.

That's it! There's nothing more to be done, either with my hair or the evening ahead of me. God save the Queen!

As she left her room and started down the staircase, she heard her name shouted until the hallway echoed. She was greeted by an exuberant Rhys, running up the stairs to grab her in his arms. "My *mus!* You are a vision! The land of the Vikings has nurtured an English princess. Even your freckles are royal!" And he kissed her nose.

Carol laughed and the dark thoughts disappeared in the ebullience of the irrepressible Rhys. He certainly did not let the past get in the way of the present. But even as she thought this, she smelled the liquor on his breath.

Rhys ushered her down the stairs like some kind of prize he had earned and awarded to himself. Lisle ran out to meet them at the bottom of the stairs dressed in blue jeans and a ski jersey. Rhys spun Carol around in front of her.

"See, Lisle! A princess, ya? She has invaded our shores and conquered us all! Doesn't she look like an English princess?"

Lisle said noncommittally, "Nice."

Rhys laughed and ruffled his sister's hair. "Lisle is indifferent to clothing. She thinks if one cannot skate in it, it is no good."

Lisle punched Rhys in the stomach and a brief wrestling match between them ensued. *How good they are together,* Carol thought. *There is real affection, with no strain. It is a family, and I wish I were a part of it.*

There was a movement at the end of the hall, and Carol turned to see Inga bustling toward them. Carol was so glad to see her that she threw out her arms and they embraced like long-lost friends.

"Inga! I didn't know you were here. I'm so glad to see you, and so sorry about . . ."

Inga grinned and gave Carol's cheek a healthy pinch. "*Oof da,* I was so mad on you! Run off in the night and hurt yourself in the troll mountains! You listen to Inga from now!"

"I promise, Inga. I wouldn't have survived without your coffee and cookies!"

"I think you survive better than you think. Now, go in for supper, or all my good food will go cold."

There was no ceremony of drinks before dinner. Inga waved Rhys, Lisle and Carol into the dining room. Mor and Grete were there, arranging candles on the table. The babble of warm trivia was simple and comfortable. Then there was a silence, and Tor entered with Solveig clinging to his arm.

Carol's determined reserve crumbled. The sight of him attached to Solveig Folkdahl immobilized her. She hoped the frozen smile on her face had some semblance of sincerity as she faced them.

They were a striking couple, beautifully blond, handsome, strong. Carol felt tiny and unkempt, even dowdy, in spite of her pretty dress and Rhys' opinion. There was no way she could compete.

Solveig greeted her crisply. Carol felt Tor's eyes on her, but she could not, would not, look into his. Tor held his mother's chair, seating her at one end of the oval table, then seated Solveig at his right on the other end. Rhys claimed a place on Tor's left, next to Carol, and Lisle plopped down without ceremony next to Solveig and opposite Carol. As dinner conversation began, Lisle caught Carol's eye and, hiding her face from the others, mouthed "Sardine Queen," making a fish-face and crossing her eyes. Carol quickly raised her napkin to her face and coughed. A good deal of the tension left her, but she would have to avoid looking at Lisle if she were not to make a fool of herself at this meal. At least she had two friends here, Lisle and Rhys—one a child and the other less than sober—but still, friends.

Inga and Grete were in their element, not only because there were guests, but because the whole family was present. Inga announced this fact with great satisfaction a number of times.

As heaping platters, steaming and fragrant, began to arrive from the kitchen, Lisle wailed, "Here it comes the feast! When it is that the sons are home, Grete and Inga sweats to make the best. That happens never else!"

"Shush, Lisle," said her mother, gentle in reproof. "They need to taste real food once in a while."

"Plain, honest food!" chimed Inga, scurrying out for another platter.

Lisle was not to be silenced. "See, Carol, flaked cod— Tor could ate a mountain of it. And meatballs in the sour cream. I knew it! As soon as Rhys steps on the door, Grete starts to make a meatball."

"Lisle," broke in Rhys, "you are in training to be a skater, but I am in training to be a meatball. Pass that platter."

As plates began to fill, Lisle held up her hand for quiet. "I want you all to knowing I am falling off my diet. Tor, please put three potatoes, many carrots and cods on my plate. I will pour the melted butter over it all to drown the guilt. Is right, 'guilt'? Carol, please to do the same and we grow fat together!"

The table settled into dinner conversation. At first, Rhys dominated, teasing and joking with his mother and Lisle, flirting outrageously with Carol. Mrs. Christiansen seemed more tolerant than amused at his antics, no doubt used to them. Lisle was delighted with every utterance Rhys made—clearly she adored him. Solveig smiled a set smile between tiny mouthfuls. Tor ate silently.

"Rhys," said his mother, "talk less and eat more. You look thin and gray." Rhys laughed and did pause in his monologue long enough to fork some food into his mouth.

In that brief silence, Carol heard Solveig's voice in a low tone, speaking Norwegian quietly, persistantly to Tor. Carol looked at the beautiful couple. Tor's face was impassive, his eyes concentrated on the plate in front of him. Solveig seemed to be trying to persuade Tor to do something. Her hand would reach out to touch his sometimes, drawing his eyes to her for a moment. He said little, occasionally nodding his head.

Tor seemed so tired. His eyes were clouded, lifeless. And the laugh lines around his eyes were merely lines, aging him. Carol felt a rush of feeling for him, wanting to hold him, comfort him, let him rest in her arms . . . wanting to protect him from the attentions of Solveig Folkdahl. But of course she didn't know if he wanted protection, nor if he needed comfort, nor certainly if he would take them from her weak arms.

Suddenly the voice of Helge Christiansen forcefully interrupted her musing. "You speak no Norwegian, Carol?"

"No, and I'm embarrassed. You all speak English so well."

"Then we must all speak it at all times in your presence, for it would be rude to do otherwise." She seemed to be directing her remark to Lisle, but everyone at the table surely knew she referred to Solveig. Carol could not control a glance at the elegant woman and found with some satisfaction a slight flush on the forehead of the pale face. To Carol's surprise, there seemed to be a ghost of a smile on Tor's face. Mor continued, "Do you understand, Lisle?"

Lisle protested. "Why do you telling me? I am speaking English to Carol all the long!"

Mor answered, "And very bad English, I notice." She turned to Carol. "You are not hungry, Carol?"

"I . . . actually, I've eaten a great deal. Everything is so fresh and delicious. But I'm afraid my mind was wandering."

"Pleasant wanderings, I hope?"

"Oh, yes! So much is new to me. It's hard to absorb it all so quickly."

"You and I must take some time to become acquainted. I'm sorry I have not seen to your comfort as I should have."

"Not at all! I've been very comfortable, and appreciate being in your home. I feel that I'm imposing, that I should really be in a hotel. After all, I'm just here to work, and you weren't expecting me . . ."

"No, no. Too much work destroys the soul. Life is much too short. After dinner, you will please join me for a long coffee in my rooms."

Rhys protested, "But Mor, I hoped to take Carol out dancing tonight, to show her Bergen! Since I'm sure Tor hasn't bothered with the minor matters of mere pleasure. . ."

Tor's eyes blazed across the table at his brother, but Mor broke in. "I will not take the whole evening. You will have time to play after Carol and I have a cup of coffee."

Carol's evening seemed to have been decided for her, and now she was caught in a new part of this family's tensions. Mrs. Christiansen seemed to be less than warm toward Solveig, even though Solveig's place at her table was clearly established. It was odd, and Carol wondered whether it would become clear to her when she joined Helge for coffee, whether some hidden agenda would be revealed . . . Carol dismissed her ominous thoughts. The woman was just being gracious. But they crept in again. Perhaps this matriarch thought Rhys' flirtatious attention to her was suspicious. That couldn't be, for surely Rhys flirted with everyone. Or perhaps Mrs. Christiansen wondered about the time she and Tor had spent on the way to Bergen, though that was clearly labeled as work. There would be no way for her to know what had passed between Carol and Tor that afternoon. The questions she asked herself did not clarify anything. There was nothing to do but wait and see what the coffee hour would bring.

After dinner, Rhys disappeared with Lisle, promising to be back in an hour to take Carol out. Mrs. Christiansen took Carol familiarly by the arm, and they left the dining room, passing Solveig's brittle smile. She felt Tor rise as they passed, his eyes on her. Carol was relieved to get out of that room, away from both of them.

In Mrs. Christiansen's suite of rooms, comfortable and cozy with remembrances, Carol felt more at ease than she had in hours. They seated themselves in front of a glowing fire to take the chill off the night air. The coffee was delicious, and Mrs. Christiansen seemed to be at ease with her. Her questions were friendly, casual—about her life in England, her interests and friends, her impressions of Norway.

"I haven't led a very exciting life, I'm afraid. I've never had a chance . . . no, that's not true. I've never *taken* a chance!" Carol said, feeling apologetic about that fact in the presence of a woman who had lived so vitally, so physically.

"But you are very young. Life is hard for the young, I

think. There are so many questions, so many problems. If there are not enough problems, we can be sure the young will invent some."

Carol agreed with a rueful laugh. "I'm sure I'm guilty of that, for I seem to see problems wherever I look. I'm probably imagining every one of them." Carol felt an impulse to tell her everything she was feeling, everything she had felt in the last few days. But common sense told her that any emotional outburst would surely offend the woman, certainly since the matters touched those she loved. Besides, Carol had never poured her soul out to anyone. She would not know how to begin.

Mrs. Christiansen put down her cup and folded her hands in front of her, a look of quiet decision on her face. She spoke softly.

"My children too have problems. They are very different from each other. They came to me so far apart; it is as if they grew up in an entirely different generation. Lisle will survive well. She is strong in many ways, thinks more deeply than can be seen in her behavior. She also has a sense of humor, and a sense of what is real and what is sham. Rhys has that gift too, but he wastes it—laughing without feeling. I fear for him."

She paused, staring into her second son's future with sadness. "Anyone who hopes for a life with Rhys has much disappointment in store. He is like the froth on the sea waves, lively and dancing but made of bubbles."

"And Tor?" Carol could have bitten her tongue for her anxious request, her too obvious interest.

Mor looked at her sharply. "Tor is the sea beneath the waves. The currents are strong and treacherous. Who sails there must be a very fine sailor."

As casually as she could, Carol asked, "Is Solveig a good sailor?"

"Solveig does everything well."

Carol's heart sank. "Yes, I can see that. I hope . . . they'll be very happy together."

Mor stared into the glowing fire. "Do they seem happy to you now? Solveig and Tor?"

Carol looked away. "They make a very attractive couple."

"Yes, they do. Our two families go back a long way. But I ask you again if they seem happy?"

How could Carol dare to tell this concerned, loving mother that she thought her son the most unhappy, tortured man she had ever known? How could she say she had never seen Tor and Solveig smile at each other or even pass an affectionate glance between them? "I don't know them very well, of course. They are a handsome pair, and I'm sure Miss Folkdahl will make him a very good wife."

Mor looked directly into Carol's eyes. "She will make him a terrible wife, and neither one of them will ever admit it. Equally stubborn, ever since they were children."

Carol couldn't respond. She could not reveal her true feelings, and the woman clearly saw through her polite evasions. She remained silent for a moment, then asked, "The American girl, Joleen?"

The older woman sighed. "That might have been, if the girl had only . . ."

Carol waited for the end of the sentence. Had only what? Lived?

But Mor rose from her chair, the interview at an end. "I keep you too long from your evening. You are good to spend time with an old woman when there is so much young life outside."

Carol protested sincerely, taking the woman's hand. "It's a privilege to know you, Mrs. Christiansen, and I'm afraid it's your time that's wasted on someone like me."

"Someone like you?" The woman's hands were big and strong around her own. "I believe you do not know yourself. Be patient with us, with my sons. And call me 'Helge' from now on, to please me."

Carol went out of the room feeling warmed by the woman's confidence and friendliness, yet confused by the purpose of it all. But perhaps there was no "purpose." Perhaps it was just as she said . . . a friendly visit.

She could not face an evening with Rhys, and he hadn't really asked her. He had simply assumed she would go with him. She decided to plead a headache and went down the stairs to look for him. She heard voices in the living room and went in through the open door.

They were all there—Rhys, Solveig, Lisle and Tor. They looked up when she entered, and there was a questioning look on each face, as though they were waiting for some kind of revelation or verdict. Even Tor searched her face. Rhys spoke first.

"You have survived! Congratulations, my *mus*!"

Carol stared at him, wondering what she was supposed to have survived. Had she undergone a test without knowing? Was there another game she had been forced to play without knowing the rules?

Lisle ran to her, took her hands and dragged her to the sofa. "Rhys is tease!" Lisle considered the word. "It is correct—tease?"

Carol laughed as she sat down next to Lisle. "Yes, it is very correct. But tell me, what is it that I've survived?"

Lisle said, "I do not know. But everyone has been walking about on the eggs since you went up to Mor. I say is silly. I talk to Mor every day, and no one walks on the eggs for me!"

Solveig sat down on the other side of Lisle and hugged the girl. Carol thought she saw the skater pull back just a little, though she said nothing. Solveig smiled and patted Lisle's knee. "So, you race on Friday? I will come to cheer you on. Luckily, I plan to stay in Bergen for a few days."

Lisle smiled thinly. "That will be very nice." Then she leapt up and ran to Tor. "Tor, you be there too. You promised!"

Tor barely glanced at her. "I promised no such thing,

Lisle. If all is going well, I will try, but I cannot promise."

Lisle let out a feline yowl at Tor, then butted her head against his chest and began pummeling him. "You must come! You must! I beat you to death if you don't!"

With lightning quickness, Tor bent down, lifted the girl over his shoulder and threatened her with a brisk spanking. He held her high, like a weightless ornament, her arms flailing uselessly. "Wait! You are too old to be spanked, but just the right age for the tickling torture!" Lisle screamed with delight as she was dumped on the carpet and tickled mercilessly.

"Stop, Tor, stop! Or I will pour molasses in your ski boots!"

"You already did that, Lisle, when you were six! I have not forgotten!" Tor scooped up an armful of pillows and piled them on top of the wriggling, giggling form of Lisle.

Carol laughed and applauded. The sight of the playful Tor was so natural, so easy. And she shared Lisle's joy at her big brother's attention. Solveig looked uncomfortable at so much exuberance. Rhys laughed too, but it was a strange laugh, a puzzled one. Tor was a man whose attitudes changed like quicksilver. Carol saw the man who had laughed with her about trolls on the mountain, and this teasing, rough-housing man was the same, a man with a vital capacity for love and fun. But she knew the man Rhys knew and what she had seen in his cold forbidding mood was even more real.

Lisle escaped from her mound of pillows and screamed her way out of the room, Tor pursuing her to the doorway. Rhys made a movement, just a gesture, to take up the chase, but at that moment Tor turned back into the room with a face of granite. Rhys stared at his brother for a moment, then whirled around to Carol.

Pulling her to her feet, Rhys forced a smile. "Enough of family! Come, the night is young but aging quickly! We will dance all the night long!"

Carol gently disengaged herself from his grasp. "I'll

sorry, Rhys, but I don't feel very well. Just a headache. I haven't been able to catch up on my sleep for several days. I would doze off on the dance floor, I'm sure."

Solveig said, "What is this? You are rejecting Rhys Christiansen? The matriarchal conference was a success!"

Rhys glared and spat out, "You assume too much, Solveig. If Carol rejects me, perhaps Mor was not able to persuade her that I am the supreme catch of *Norge!*"

Solveig looked up into the rafters and said, "If you are the supreme catch of *Norge,* I am the Goddess Freya!"

"Yes, Solveig, you are a fisher, not a fish."

"Very true, Rhys."

Rhys opened his arms wide to Solveig. "Catch me then, the rejected suitor."

Solveig turned to Carol. "Only Carol can say whether you are rejected, not your mother."

So that was why they had all been waiting for her return from the visit with Mor! They considered her a prospect for a serious relationship with Rhys! It couldn't be. And the talk she had with Helge did not indicate anything of the kind. Or had it? That remark about Rhys being the foam on the waves . . . perhaps it had been meant to discourage Carol from pursuing her second son.

Rhys had dismissed Solveig—rather reluctantly, Carol thought—and was trying to persuade Carol to reconsider an evening out with him, his words and teasing smile obstructing her attempt at analysis. And then Solveig joined in the persuasion, encouraging her to accompany Rhys. "Only so she can be alone with Tor!" thought Carol. And in the same instant she condemned her own pettiness.

Finally Tor broke in firmly. "If Miss Smythe is unwilling to go out, it is rude to insist." The bantering left off immediately. Tor turned to Carol. "If I kept you at work too long this afternoon, I apologize. You must please tell me when you are tired."

Carol dared to look into his eyes for a long moment,

and she knew she hoped for some sign of real caring. But there was nothing there but polite, disinterested concern. Had he forgotten what had occurred between them? Didn't it matter to him whether or not she went dancing with his brother . . . to be in his brother's arms when his had held her so tightly? She had so many questions and no answers.

She said her good nights and left them. She had the strange sensation that the three people she had left in the room were more alone, more isolated from each other, than they were from her.

She stripped off her clothes and fell into the depths of the feather bed. Her sleep was deep. Her dreams were of mountain storms and warm caresses and Tor Christiansen.

Chapter Eight

WHEN SHE AWOKE in the morning, Carol had the headache she had pretended to have the night before. But after a shower she felt better and almost ready to face another day in close proximity to Tor.

There was an elaborate breakfast laid out in the empty dining room, coffee cakes and a variety of cheese and thinly sliced smoked meats. *English breakfasts are supposed to be enormous,* she thought, *but after this I shall be able to climb the cliffs of the fjords.*

Helge soon joined her, apologizing for not being there to greet her. "We all have such different schedules in the morning. Lisle is already at practice and Tor at work. He always starts very early. He said he would send a car for you in about fifteen minutes." She paused and smiled at Carol. "And of course Rhys is still asleep. The two of you must have had a very late night. I hope he didn't tire you too much?"

"I didn't go with Rhys last night. A nagging headache persuaded me to get a good long sleep. I suppose he found some friends. I hope so."

Helge's smile faded. "I'm sorry you weren't with him. He would be in good hands with you, I think."

Carol managed a weak smile and concentrated on buttering a thick wedge of fresh coffee cake, redolent with almond.

Helge said, "But people are what they want to be, and no one else can do anything about it, ya?"

Carol was not sure Helge wanted agreement. There was

a suggestion of a plea in her voice, but Carol did agree with her about changing people. If she were able to make him happier with himself, she would be glad to try. But Rhys seemed satisfied, and Carol was not sure she would want to change anyone as bright and enthusiastic as he, however much the enthusiasm might be pretended. His mother stood quietly, waiting for a response.

A blare of a car horn interrupted them. Carol gulped down a last swallow of coffee, smiled a cheerful, non-committal goodbye to Helge, gathered her handbag and ran out the front door. When she saw the MG parked outside with the engine running, her heart skipped a beat. Tor had come for her himself. But the voice that wished her a formal good morning was that of Solveig Folkdahl.

"Tor asked me to drop you off at his office."

"It's very kind of you. I hope this doesn't inconvenience you—keep you from your work, I mean."

Solveig smiled at her. Apparently the evening with Tor had reassured her. "Not at all. I come and go as I please. It is not difficult when one is the president of one's own company."

Carol smiled back. "I envy you." And she thought, *More than you know.*

Solveig shoved the car into gear and pressed the accelerator. The car lurched forward, and Carol cringed in sympathy for the finely-tuned engine.

They spoke of nothing consequential the rest of the route. Solveig indicated points of interest with an admirable sense of national pride. Carol stared out the window, stilling any questions that came to her about the city. She wouldn't admit that Solveig had superior knowledge or claim on even the scenery. Her natural curiosity was obliterated by other questions from her self-admitted jealousy. *Where did you sleep last night? With Tor? How else did you get his car? Why should I care!?*

Solveig drove up to the entrance of a large office building proclaimed as "North Sea Petroleum" by the familiar swirling blue design, and dropped Carol off without ceremony. The woman drove off, but her presence inside the building continued in the design, the "Frigid Folkdahl Look," as Carol christened it. She shivered and admonished herself for her pettiness.

A jolly little secretary greeted her with great solicitousness, offering her services at any time, apologizing for her English, which Carol found excellent, and ceremoniously guiding her on a tour of the offices. The other workers seemed friendly but curiously shy. *I believe they think I'm someone important,* she thought. *This certainly has a V.I.P. feeling about it.* She didn't know quite how to act, never having been singled out for special attention of any kind. It was pleasantly strange, and she thought it must be that she was a foreign visitor. But she hoped that Tor had given orders.

They finally reached an office that the secretary said was to be Carol's. "The Ballinger material has been laid out for you. Please let me know if there is anything I can do for you. If Mr. Christiansen is unable to escort you to lunch, I would be most honored if you will accompany me."

Carol thanked her as she bowed out, trying to be the very important person that apparently she was supposed to be. It was a bit of a relief to see the secretary close the door.

The office was sterile, but the wide windows looked down on a flower market that blazed with color. Lush bouquets arranged on tiered steps seemed to cascade down like a block-long waterfall of color. It would be a welcome visual escape when the office walls closed in.

The files were neatly arranged on the vast surface of the pale beechwood desk. She saw new notes that Tor had made on the top sheet of paper. The strong, broad strokes of his pen stood out with bold authority amid the smudged scribbles of Mr. Ballinger. Carol felt a tremor in the pit of her stomach. Would they be working together, or would the sleek blond office be hers alone? There had not been a moment alone with him since their work session in his study; no chance to talk, no way to guess his feelings about the long, intense kiss that had intruded on their work.

He's probably forgotten all about it, she thought. But a growing sense of dread filled her at the thought of being alone with him. *Are you afraid something will happen? Or are you afraid nothing will happen?*

Finally she spoke to herself aloud, "Pull yourself together! You've got several days of work to face with the man, and this roller-coaster of romantic nonsense has to stop!"

By the time Tor came into the office, she was in control, and the sight of him did not weaken her will. His attitude helped, for he was distant and businesslike. They plotted the sequence of the remaining work and estimated that a Saturday evening deadline was feasible.

Carol said, "Then I'll make arrangements for my return flight to London for Sunday morning, if that will be convenient."

Silence greeted this statement. Carol looked into his eyes and found that they seemed puzzled. Did he think she would stay in Bergen forever? Perhaps she imagined it, but he hesitated for a long moment before he answered.

"Of course. You may call from here. Also, you may want to call McKinzie. He would probably appreciate knowing about our progress and your return as well." And Tor rose and left the office.

Carol breathed a sigh of relief at his departure, annoyed that she had been more tense than she had realized. She made the calls immediately, first to a commercial airline, then to Mr. McKinzie in London.

"I thought you'd died and gone to Valhalla, or whatever the dickens they call it!" The sound of his voice brought her back to solid ground more firmly than anything she had experienced since she left English soil. "That lunatic, Ballinger, you know, he's well on his way to recovery. He'll be back to drive us bats as hatters in a month. The Lord save us from all geniuses!"

Carol carefully described what she was doing and how far along the transcription had come. McKinzie seemed satisfied that the work was progressing and encouraged her to take her time. "Public relations is vital too, my girl, so apply some stick 'em wherever we need it. Do it up right, and know that I'm appreciating everything you're doing up there on that God-forsaken glacier! And keep your feet warm!"

Carol laughed as she hung up the phone. She believed that McKinzie really did care about keeping her feet warm.

The next three days seemed disjointed. The hours flew by and the minutes crept. No day had a steady, routine flow. Tor was not with her very much as the remaining files needed more translation than analysis. But when he was with her, working over a particularly difficult section, an hour was interminable. Minute by minute her resolve crumbled as she felt his warmth near her own, as his breath touched her hair. Minute by minute she would mount her defenses against her response to him. She thought of her pleasure when she had imagined she could read his moods, for it had been imagination. At times she felt she was an embarrassment to him, then he seemed to treat her as some kind of time bomb about to detonate, splattering stories of lofts and car wrecks about his controlled, neat offices. But most of the time, it was all business.

Escaping from the office at lunch time, sometimes with other office personnel, more often alone, her explorations diverted her with the charm and fascinations of Bergen. The twelfth century buildings, the twisting, narrow streets,the craft and antique stores were all compelling. She almost ran from street to street, feeling teased with glimpses of the life of the city, feeling time slipping away from her.

Her evenings were very quiet. Rhys had gone back to Oslo and wouldn't return until Friday for Lisle's race. Lisle was consumed with preparations for the race, and Tor was simply absent, though she felt his presense in the house at night. She and Helge joined Inga and Grete in the kitchen for the evening meal, passing the time with enthusiastic discussions about food.

Carol found herself looking forward to the after-dinner talks with Helge. There were no more revelatory or challenging conversations, no feeling of mystery about them. Helge seemed more open and free, gradually beginning to speak of her past—of ships and sailing and the vigorous, physical life she had led. There was no sadness in her stories, no regrets, neither for the dangers nor the losses. Helge Christiansen was a woman who had been challenged, had taken risks, had loved and lived with energy and resilience. Yet still there was a hard edge to her voice when she spoke of the sea that had taken her husband from her.

On Friday morning, she walked into her office and was greeted with a blaze of color. It was as if the flower market below had been moved into the room. Its sterile symmetry was totally destroyed with baskets of vibrant yellows, pinks and purples—flowers of every size and kind filling every surface and nearly every foot of floor space. A carefully lettered note displayed on the one of the baskets read, "From Rhys Christiansen, who desires your flowering presence at dinner this evening."

Carol laughed aloud at the joyous excessiveness of the gesture. And at that moment Tor entered the office.

His normal, serious frown changed to a look of confusion for a moment. He stared at her. Carol waved the note weakly and said, "Rhys has apparently decided I should work in a garden."

Tor said, "Rhys' idea of beauty is excessive and extravagant," and he went on, almost too quietly for her to hear, "It is not as beautiful as our meadow."

Had she heard correctly? Had he said "our" meadow? Did he remember that afternoon in the mountains as beautiful?

Immediately his manner changed and he addressed her formally. "The work goes well?"

"Yes, very well. If there are no complications, I think only a few more hours of work will complete everything."

"Then perhaps you will like to attend Lisle's race this afternoon? I find I am able to be free also."

"Wonderful, thanks so much! And Lisle will be so pleased that you can be there. It's very important to her."

He looked at her, pausing for a long moment, and said, "Yes, perhaps. You will be ready to leave at two o'clock. I will come by for you."

"I'll be ready."

Tor nodded and started to leave, then turned back to her. "Please look ahead at the remaining material today. I will be out of the office all day tomorrow."

"All day?" The question was out of her mouth before she thought. She hoped there was no hint in the words of the disappointment she felt. She knew that it didn't matter, that he paid so little attention to her anyway.

Tor continued, "I am going out to one of the rigs early in the morning. I want to examine the situation with the cables myself, and so . . ."

"Let me go with you!" Again her spontaneous wish was audible before she could consider it.

He frowned. "To the rig? It is no place for a woman. What would you do there?"

"I'd see the actual machinery!" The words came out in a rush, and she moved close to him. "Please! I've been dealing with diagrams and paper for years, and never seen one cable, one turbine, one anything! I want to see the actual operation, not all these pieces of paper. I won't get in the way, I promise. Please, Tor!"

She stopped, feeling his frown on her as much as seeing it, feeling she had gone too far, come too close. He moved away from her, his frown deepening. But his words were surprisingly positive.

"Very well. It is perhaps good for our mutual business. The practical experience is valuable, but . . ."

Carol waited for his condition. He seemed troubled, almost vulnerable. His hand reached out and absently touched a flower on her desk.

"You will not tell Mor . . . not that I go to the rig, nor that you will accompany me. My mother is wise and strong, but she hates the sea with a passion that is not reasonable. And it is better she not know I go." He turned to her and almost smiled. "The mother must worry about the children always, ya? And she would be angry if she knew that you go too. Last night, I heard her speaking to you of my father and the ships. It has been many years since she spoke of that time." He seemed about to say more but broke off, rubbing his eyes as though erasing something from his vision. "I will see you after lunch then." And he left.

When he returned for her, he seemed gentler somehow. Of course she should have expected that Solveig would go with them, but when she saw her waiting in the front seat of a company Volvo, Carol felt cheated. Why couldn't she resign herself to the fact that Solveig Folkdahl and Tor Christiansen were a couple, that their permanent relationship was inevitable? She fumed at herself and wished she were on the Sunday flight to London.

The arena was packed, the crowd intent. Several events had preceeded their arrival, and the seriousness of both crowd and participants was evidence of the event's significance. This was a matter of Nordic pride; success in the approaching Olympic Winter Games counted a great deal both internationally and personally. A hundred young athletes milled around, some happy, some glum, most in groups of intense discussion with coaches and each other. Their jackets with colorful emblems and patches blazed announcements of effort and accomplishment.

Tor guided Solveig and Carol to the box where Rhys and Helge were already seated. Carol felt pale in comparison to the other members of the party as greetings were exchanged and seats taken. Her old gray work suit could not compete. Helge's soft knit suit in light blue complemented her hearty look. Rhys was in butter soft suede slacks and matching jacket. Even Tor's severe business suit of navy set off his blue eyes and blond hair strikingly. But the jewel in the crowd was Solveig. She removed her light coat to reveal slacks and blouse of cherry red silk. Over her shoulder flowed a scarf that captured the rainbow. It seemed to Carol that the woman took an extraordinarily long time to sit down, so that the eyes of the crowd so intent on the races were distracted, at least those around them. Carol thought, *And I'm sure I provide a strong contrast, in my bright jealous green.*

Rhys claimed a seat next to Carol immediately and began commenting on everything. "Look at Mor. She is something—a Viking goddess, my mother, is she not? She does the cross-country in the winter, by herself, in the mountains."

Carol wasn't sure what cross-country was, but she assumed it meant something super-human. She tried to listen to Rhys, barely managing to insert her thanks for the flowers between his observations. She tried even harder to ignore the closeness of Tor and Solveig, seated together in front of her and Rhys. The woman just hung on him! Carol gritted her teeth and admonished herself. *He probably loved it.*

Lisle, intent and serious, appeared for her first event. The race was close, and Carol could feel her muscles contracting in empathy as Lisle, lean in the skin-tight costume, stroked strongly toward the finish line. She came in second. Carol caught some of the joy and pride in her as she waved at her family. She saw Tor and her face lit with excitement. She answered his "thumbs up" signal with a broad grin and disappeared to prepare for her next race.

Rhys was busy claiming credit. "I told her about the final sprint . . . that she must forget all control and let the ice and speed take over! The instincts must push the body!"

Tor turned to argue. "It is wrong! The last sprint must be in total control, carefully planned and followed through. It is the time to remember everything! I told her this long ago, and she followed my advice to the letter!"

Mor leaned over to her as her sons continued to argue and said quietly, "The men, they argue so foolishly . . . armchair skaters. Lisle hears them, but she listens only to her coach. Lisle learned early how to please her brothers. She nods seriously and thanks them, but seldom does what they suggest. It is silly, what we do to please men, but they will not have it any other way, ya?"

Lisle's next two events were even more exciting. She won third place in one race and first in the other by just the length of a skate. Her standings qualified her for the Norwegian Olympic skating team.

At the end of the afternoon's events, they pushed through the crowds and found Lisle, surrounded by her teammates, all of them beaming proudly. She saw them and broke away from her friends to throw herself at her family. "Thank you all for being here! It is a help that is wonderful! I can feel you all pushing me to the finish! I am so glad and happiness!"

Rhys slapped his sister on the back, and even Tor managed a smile at her. Helge hugged her and told her that gold medal would surely hang around her neck if she continued to work hard. Solveig formally shook her hand and backed away to let the family continue its little celebration, and Carol was conscious that both she and Solveig were isolated from the beautiful, loving family.

"I have to go to party," said Lisle. "It is good, ya?" Everyone agreed she must go and celebrate with every ounce of energy she might have left, which seemed to be considerable.

Lisle dashed off to join her group, and the rest of them quickly broke up. Solveig and Tor escorted Helge from the arena, and Rhys drew her in another direction, announcing their dinner plans to everyone in a thirty-meter radius. Carol glanced at the disappearing form of Tor once, then allowed herself to be guided by Rhys out of the arena.

"You need not worry, Carol," Rhys said, reading her hesitation as doubt of him. "I'll be on my best behavior. You will not know me from an Englishman with a bowler hat!"

Rhys proved to be as good as his word. The restaurant was lovely, the food wonderful, and Rhys ordered no drinks other than the bottle of wine they shared. He was attentive, considerate charming . . . and undemanding.

"The athletic hopes of the family rest on little sister. Lisle will win a gold medal in the three-mile, I am sure."

"And you, Rhys? Lisle says you are a fine skier."

"Not so very fine, I think. In any case, I quit before anyone could know whether it was true or not." He laughed, a trace of bitterness in it. "I never have to prove anything."

"But why did you quit?" Carol persisted.

A shadow crossed his face. "I am lazy, that is all. The ptarmigan was very fine, don't you think?"

"Wonderful, a bit like pheasant," said Carol, realizing Rhys was not going to discuss skiing further.

The waitress served dessert, a crystal bowl of mounded whipped cream and golden berries. Rhys served her a gigantic portion, and when she protested the amount, he said, "Shush, little *mus*. In five minutes you will ask for more."

And in five minutes she did. "What are they? I've never tasted anything so heavenly!"

"Cloud berries, the epitome of the Norwegian gastronomical experience!" And he heaped up more for both of them. "In the late summer, you and your lover go to the hills and pick the cloud berries. And it is the absolute truth that you never get any of them home, because you eat as fast as you pick. You don't even stop to make love!"

"I'm desolate that I won't experience that—neither berry-picking nor mysterious lover. My work won't keep me here another week, much less through the summer."

Rhys persisted in the story of the cloud berries. "There is no mystery. When you eat them with someone you love, the two of you remember the tasting during the long winter. It is a shame that Tor is not here to taste with you."

Carol looked at him sharply, then away as she felt the blood rise to her face. "Why on earth should Tor be here?"

"I think you understand."

"Not in the least. He isn't at all interested in me nor I in him, and he is obviously spoken for."

"You are sure of all that?"

"Of course."

"Even sure that you are not interested?"

"Absolutely, not that it's any of your business."

"Ah, but it is. Not because I pry into your life, but because I look out for the interests of my brother. And I know my brother is . . . affected by you."

"What do you mean? I've hardly seen him, hardly been with him since we arrived in Bergen. At the office, there's only work, and . . ."

"Carol, listen to me. For two years, Tor has not smiled. He has been a cold man, even a tyrant. He has taken himself away from us . . . not only from me, the profligate brother who deserves his wrath, but even from Mor and

Lisle. He is hard and indifferent to anything but North Sea Petroleum."

"It seems to me he still is."

"Shush! Let me finish. The other night, with Lisle, Tor lifted her up and laughed out loud. He was warm and foolish. I swear, Carol, that was the first time I've seen my brother really enjoy himself in a long time. Why?"

"I haven't any answers, Rhys, none."

"You may not have an answer, you may *be* an answer. There is nothing different in Tor's life, in all our lives, except you. It has to be."

Carol wanted very much to believe Rhys, to have that small hope, even if it meant only what he said—that she had made a difference in the life of Tor Christiansen. But Rhys had not seen Tor glaring at her on the roadside. Rhys had not seen the cruel kiss nor felt the icy turning away. Rhys had not witnessed hours of side-by-side labor with no smiles, no warmth, not even pleasantries. If she had made a difference in his life, it didn't seem to be for the better. The moment with Lisle was simply an aberration, which even tyrants must have sometimes.

Rhys persisted. "I know he still snarls like the wolf and freezes us all with his eyes. But even his growling is changed. The last time he shouted at me, it was with real anger, not the cold sneer he has punished me with for so long."

"Why? Why has he punished you? What did you do to him?"

"I did nothing to him. I swear to you, I did nothing."

"Then how can he treat you the way he does?"

Rhys laughed without humor. "Because I am not good enough to be his brother." He shrugged. "Because I am a drunk."

Carol reached across the table and took his hand in both of hers. She held it tightly and looked into his eyes. "You are not drunk now."

Rhys laughed the same humorless laugh. "It is true! And

I have not been drunk for three days. If this keeps up much longer, I'll forget how!" And he signaled for a waiter to bring him a brandy.

Carol hung on to his hand. "No, Rhys, please. Unless you need to forget I'm here, to escape from me."

Rhys squeezed her hand and sighed. "I'm sorry, *mus*. I do not want to escape from you. It's so easy to say 'I'm sorry' to you. I wish I could say it to my brother. But I can't tell him 'I'm sorry for what I did not do.' He will not believe."

Carol's voice was quiet, factual. "He believes you were responsible for Joleen's death."

His eyes flashed pain. "You see much. Or did my mother tell you?"

"No, she hasn't said anything. I've simply put two and two together. I'm right, aren't I?"

"Yes."

"But you weren't responsible?"

The waiter put a large brandy snifter in front of Rhys and bowed away. Rhys' lean hands wrapped tightly around it, and he stared intently into the amber smoothness.

"I was very drunk at the party." His voice was slow as he pulled the memory from deep inside himself. "Tor was out of the country, and that was convenient for Joleen and me. It was convenient for Joleen and twenty other men. And Joleen was drunk too. She was more than drunk, she was crazy! She was like a wild woman when she wasn't with Tor, sometimes even when she was with him. But he held her tighter than any of the rest of us. And when he would leave, his wild she-wolf would slip her leash, go on a rampage."

Rhys looked at Carol, his eyes begging her to under-stand, to believe. "The woman was a carnivore. She ate men alive. That night, I fell into the back seat of the car, Tor's car, a BMW much like the one he has now. Joleen drove us up into the mountains. She said she was going to find Tor's 'harbor.' I remember so little of the ride, not much more than being tossed around in the back seat like an overgrown rag doll. I remember the tires screaming on the road, the radio turned up as loud as possible, and Joleen laughing. It was very funny to her that we were going to spend the night together in Tor's precious hideaway, hilarious that we would defile his nest."

"You couldn't stop her?"

"Not even if I had been in condition to try. It didn't matter, don't you see? If I hadn't been in the car, some other man would have. It didn't matter to Joleen who was there."

"I see," said Carol quietly.

"Finally I came to some level of consciousness and tried to get her to slow down, but she wouldn't listen. She just laughed and called me a coward. I didn't care what she called me, I was frightened. Even in my stupor I had sense to be afraid. I tried to crawl over the seat to force her to stop, and she hit me with something. I think it was a whiskey bottle. Joleen was very strong, and she swung the bottle at my head with all her strength. I was stunned. I sat there, staring through the blood running down my forehead. And Joleen laughed and took both her hands off the steering wheel. I can see it, hear it, as though it were happening right now. She shouted, 'I'm going to fly over this damn mountain! Hang on, honey, here we go!' And then there was a terrible silence. I don't know how long that silence lasted, but I know I will never hear death so close again and live to tell about it."

Rhys' knuckles were white against the glass he clutched. "I came out of the wreck with a few bruises and the cut from the whiskey bottle. Joleen was killed instantly."

Carol took his hands from the glass and held them tightly, massaging the tension away from his fingers. "How horrible for you. And not your fault at all."

Rhys smiled at her weakly, exhausted from his story and the emotions it had aroused. "You think not?"

"Of course not. She must have been mad! Surely Tor

knew what she was! And when he heard your side of the story, he must have been too emotionally shocked to really understand, to really hear . . ."

"He has never heard it."

"But why? Surely it would be better for him to know the truth . . ."

"It wouldn't matter, not to Tor. You see, I was the man. I was with his woman, and I should have taken care of her. There can be no excuses, no special circumstances. I was the man. And in my brother's eyes, I am no longer a man."

"But that's not fair! How can he . . ."

Suddenly Rhys was calming her instead of the other way around. "Shush, little one. It is his way. If it were not, he would not be Tor."

Carol looked into the sad eyes of the young man and said, "You love him very much, don't you?"

Rhys looked away. "It is not talked of—love, among men."

"Well, it should be!" Carol's eyes flashed. "He should know what a burden you've been carrying. He should know how much you hurt for his sake!"

Rhys smiled at her vehemence. "You are good medicine. Good for me, and even better for Tor."

Again Carol started to protest.

"Please, Carol, believe me. And try to be patient with Tor. He has changed since you came . . . not much, but it has given me, all of us, some glimpse of the man we used to know. Oh, Tor was always serious, always worked very hard. But he played hard too, in the past . . . especially his skiing. And after the accident, he stopped, he quit. So I quit too. I did not quit because of the accident, but because of Tor. I cannot play anymore, unless I am drunk, because Tor can't. It doesn't matter for me, but it matters for my brother."

Carol couldn't argue with the pleading blue eyes. It must have taken great strength for him to say what he had, to ask of her what he had asked. She could only be silent. Certainly she could be patient, but she was no missionary. She couldn't save anybody or anything. And surely Rhys was wrong about her having caused any change in Tor. If he seemed to show some signs of coming out of his self-imposed glacier, it was simply the time for it—some mid-summer thaw that time and the elements caused, not Carol Smythe.

Rhys pushed his untouched glass away from him. There was nothing more to say . . . no promises, no future—only a secret shared. And the secret hurt them both.

They left the restaurant and started the silent drive back to the Christiansen house. Carol's mind played and re-played the same phrase, *I'll go back to London Sunday, back to London Sunday* . . .

Rhys said a pleasant good night to her at the bottom of the stairs. As she started up to her room, she heard the front door open and close. Apparently Rhys was not able to end his evening so early. She hoped he would not drink too much. *But why should I trouble myself? Why should I involve my heart with these strangers, just because my work has thrust me into their midst?*

She sat on her bed for a time, staring idly around the room. The menagerie of trolls arranged on her table stared back at her. They seemed less quaint, less charming than they had in the full sun on the mountain. The carved eyes peered at her, questioning, perhaps promising something, something evil. *I'm getting the crawling creeps!* she thought and resolved to end her mood with the best medicine—work. It was early and she felt confined, rest-less. She rose briskly and started down the stairs with coffee and accomplishment in mind.

A hot mug of fresh coffee at her side, Carol opened the last file, which she had brought with her in hopes of some idle moments on the trip to the rig in the morning. She read the title, "Pentagon Rigs; Struts and Braces." Carol stared at Ballinger's scribbles, which filled every available space around the drawing. Tor had not touched the papers; there was no sign of his pen. Perhaps he hadn't even read them, and she wouldn't blame him if he hadn't tried.

As she began to work, the facts and figures gradually edged the human matters from her mind. All of her energies were focused on understanding, transcribing the pages in front of her. She typed rapidly, ordering and organizing the scrawls representing the complex calculations—stress, welds, currents . . .

It was late when the last page was neatly completed. She placed the file in the center of Tor's desk and felt the satisfaction of finishing a job. But that feeling led to another, which set off a third. Carol stood there, staring down at Tor's desk, in Tor's study, in Tor's house—and the tears started to roll down her cheeks. Angrily she brushed them away and ran out of the study and up to her room. There in the deep comfort of the feather bed, the anger left her and she sobbed uncontrollably. She wasn't sure why, or even for whom she was crying. At last she fell into a light, troubled sleep, her dreams an olio of wooden trolls marching about the room, rigid and unfeeling, toward the woman in the bed.

Chapter Nine

SATURDAY DAWNED BRIGHT and clear. Carol was awake, trying to make her swollen eyes less troll-like, when Grete tapped on her door. The crying had released some of her frustration, and she felt much better. She dressed in layers, heavy slacks and three sweaters, assuming that the trip to the rig would involve climbing about in brisk sea winds. Grete and Inga were busy elsewhere in the house, so Carol didn't have to answer questions as to why her work day was beginning so early. She ate a quick and solitary breakfast in the kitchen, growing more and more excited about the day ahead—a trip into unknown territory. She heard Tor call from the hallway, gulped her coffee, and went to meet him.

He was dressed in rough cords and a heavy sweater. Over his arm were two bright yellow slickers. With the barest of morning amenities, he tossed her one of them and went out the door. She followed, annoyed at his manner but a bit relieved that she would only have to deal with the arrogant Tor, not the one that threw her emotions into turmoil. *Forget about the guide,* she told herself, *and enjoy the tour.*

They drove to a heliport where a glistening silver helicopter awaited them, blades whirring. Carol had a moment of trepidation as she viewed the dragonfly fragility of the craft and was deafened by the shattering noise, but she steeled herself and climbed aboard. She had barely buckled herself in before the helicopter lifted off with a lurch that left her stomach some thirty feet below. Tor didn't seem to notice. He screamed at her, "First we go to Stavanger." There was no need or possibility of any further conversation.

The dragonfly-flight, a continual series of dips and whirls, ended none too quickly for Carol. After it, she knew she would find an airplane ride smooth as glass.

From the heliport in Stavanger, an American jeep drove them quickly through the boom town toward the sea. Everywhere there were buildings being erected, others torn down. Heavy machinery loaded and dumped, criss-crossing their path at every turn. Men shouted and hurried about with an urgency born of invention and need and, probably, greed. Stavanger was the land center of the entire North Sea drilling operation.

At last they reached the dock and climbed aboard a sturdy, heavily-engined boat, cast off and headed out to sea. Carol tried to stay out of the way as the sailors went about their tasks. She put on the yellow slicker to protect herself against the salt spray. She gradually became aware of the eyes of the sailors seeking her out. She found this very curious as she certainly couldn't be much to look at—a shiny yellow blob. *Sailors!* She thought, and accepted that stereotype as the reason for their attention.

Tor was busy conferring with the captain. *At least he's not hovering about as he did on the ferry. Maybe he trusts me not to fall overboard by now, or maybe he doesn't care one way or the other.*

She stood on the deck facing the bow, secure near the cabin but with a wide view of the open sea. She could feel the power of the boat as it struggled against the angry swells. Tor strode past without noticing her, his legs steady on the rolling deck, his eyes forward, his hair blowing wildly in the wind. He planted himself at the very tip of the boat and stood, arms akimbo, as though daring the rolling sea to disturb his stance.

Carol was drawn toward him. She inched her way along the rail to his side and stood there silently, facing the sea he faced. He did not look at her, and she thought he didn't know she was there beside him. She felt the rolling of the sea beneath her, rising and falling with a strong, regular rhythm, the giant pulse of the sea god. She let go of the rail and rode as Tor rode, standing free, allowing the waves to lift her, leaning against them in balance, feeling the power of the water and her own against it.

His voice bit into her as he shouted above the wind, "You are foolish to let go of the rail." He did not look at her, but his voice slapped her with physical force. Her concentration lost, she stumbled, and he immediately caught her arm and steadied her. "You see! You cannot trust the sea for a moment. It is always hungry and waits for the careless sailor to fall. This is too dangerous for you. We should have taken the helicopter directly to the rig, but I had business with the boat's captain. Go into the cabin!"

Carol didn't reply, refusing to answer his insult, embarrassed that she had again opened herself to his ridicule. Her sense of joy in the sea, of a new sensation, was destroyed. She was angry. She let go of the rail again defiantly, then turned away and walked aft, striding surely and without any hesitation away from him. She turned around the cabin, sure she was out of his sight, and grabbed a rail again. She knew her free walk away was a childish demonstration, but she had to do it, had to show him. She glared into the wake of the boat, the churning water a complement to her feelings.

She didn't know how long she stood there, becoming almost mesmerized by wind and water. It was cold, but going inside seemed a sign of weakness. After a while, she moved a bit to find a more sheltered spot. Perhaps she should go inside. There was no sense in catching pneumonia over a matter of a little pride.

She looked forward then, and suddenly it was there—the rig! It rose out of the water like some giant steel sea monster. It grew and grew as the boat plowed nearer, larger than anything Carol had ever imagined, erect and tall, incredible. She gasped in her excitement. Photographs couldn't begin to do justice to its enormity or complexity.

We make this, she thought, *in our gray offices in the middle of London! We designed this mammoth piece of machinery, this marvel!* Her heart saluted little Mr. Ballinger with his bits of paper and scrawls. *I'm proud to be a part of this,* she thought and smiled into the wind.

Their boat was swallowed by the enormous structure, the craft making a smooth entry to the interior dock and being lashed quickly and securely by the sailors and what seemed like swarms of men appearing on the rig all around them.

She followed Tor and stood for the first time on the rig. It felt steady under her feet after the heaving of the boat, but she felt the throb of engines and was reminded that this was not dry land, merely an island imposed on the angry sea by men.

Tor's reception was businesslike, without fanfare of any kind. Most of the men who greeted him were as large as he, as muscular. Their faces were leathered and ruddy with a coarse, handsome strength in each of them. They seemed not to notice the wind whipping around them.

A sudden gust tore the hood of her slicker from her head, and Carol's hair danced in the wind. Immediately she sensed a change, a silence all around her. She looked up and saw the eyes of a dozen men focused on her puzzled eyes. Then there was one long whistle, and a dozen wide grins appeared. She smiled back, feeling very female.

Tor glanced at her and mumbled something to an enormous, grinning man who seemed to be in charge. "Miss Smythe, this is Ole Jenks, the Chief Engineer. He will see to a tour of the premises for you. Ole, this is Miss Carol Smythe, representing McKinzie Marine."

Before Ole had a chance to reply, a chorus of shouts went up all around them.

"I'll show her the rig, Ole!"

"No, me! She reminds me of my sister!"

"You haven't got a sister!"

"I'll get one!"

"Ole, you owe me one!"

"I'll give her a grand tour, Ole. It'll take two or three months!"

Carol laughed aloud. There was good-natured fun in all the eyes that met hers. Ole put his arm protectively around Carol and said, "If the boss weren't here, I'd take you myself, but one of these loudmouths will have to do." He pointed at a burly, grinning man with the reddest face Carol had ever seen. "Alamo! She's yours. Touch one hair on her head, and I'll feed you to the whales!"

Alamo whooped like an Indian in an American Western film and proudly took his place beside her. When several others protested and offered to be assistant guides, Ole laughed and nodded, and soon she was surrounded. Carol glanced at Tor, but he turned away and started talking intently to Ole. Carol had no time to dwell on his indifference, for she was almost swept away by the enthusiastic men around her.

"They call me 'Alamo' because I can hold the beer fort until everybody else passes out," her guide explained. "I'm a Texan."

"He thinks that means something," jibed another fellow, "as if anybody couldn't tell when he opens his big yap."

Most of the men spoke English, and the variety of accents and idioms made their conversation an international melange. The flat Texas twang mixed with the rolling cadences of the American South, the jerks and starts

145

of the English Midlands, the lilts of Scotland and Scandinavia. The bantering and arguing that went on was clearly for her benefit, and there were even occasional technical explanations of the premises.

It was fascinating. The rig was really two separate structures. One was the actual drilling rig, the other the living and recreational facilities for the men. It was the latter, the "flotel," that they toured first. It was elaborate, even elegant. The flotel was complete with over three hundred beds, a comfortable dining room, a theater, even a gymnasium. The care of the workers, these men who had to spend so much time isolated at sea, had been planned thoroughly and with no expense spared. Carol knew that these were not empty luxuries. Men who worked long hours separated for long periods of time from friends and family needed to see a film once in a while, to play cards or read, to have a game of American basketball in the gymnasium.

When the tour group had examined the entire flotel, her guides were ready to retire to the lounge for refreshment before returning to work.

"Oy wager you've not 'ad a decent cup of tea since you come to Norway!"

"Tea! This girl needs a beer."

"Aye, you can tell by the look of her she's a beer drinker."

"*Nye*! She vants wodka!"

Carol laughingly broke into their argument. "Please, I'm not thirsty for anything at all, and I haven't seen the actual rig. Ah don' mind a bit."

"The rig? It's just a lot of machinery."

"I know, but please. It's the rig I really want to see."

Alamo announced in an exaggerated Texas twang, "Ya'll sit around boozin' wa'al ah take the little lady around the rig. Ah don' mind a bit."

146

A chorus of protests arose, and the entire group marched off to continue the tour.

The rig was indeed "a lot of machinery," but Carol began to recognize certain pieces, sketches and scrawls coming into her mind as she looked at the actual working elements. She was led through the inner workings of the entire structure, winding around throbbing motors and pumps in the engine room, pausing to stare at cables of immense girth, then down through shafts and a maze of intricate wires and conduits. She touched the steel, sometimes hot, sometimes icy cold to her fingers. In everything she could feel the vibration, the tension of the metal itself. It seemed alive beneath her hands.

The men on duty at the machinery were happy to pause for Carol's excited questions, charmed by her enthusiasm and surprised by her knowledge. It was all "book larnin'," as Alamo observed, but her questions obviously impressed even him. Her excitement blended with their own pride and interest in their work, in this new frontier of labor, of exploration, of danger.

"Heck, sure it's dangerous. What ain't?"

"Better than sitting around some office wearing a necktie."

"And we got fresh air . . . none of that lousy pollution."

Carol was beginning to feel a bit queasy from the stench of oil fumes, but she didn't comment on the man's opinion.

"The cables," she said, "are a problem sometimes, aren't they?"

"Wa'll, they're doin' their job now—just get a li'l quiverin' once in a while. Nothin' we can do about it."

"The cables are fine; it's the confounded sea that's the problem!"

"Yeah, Neptune keeps stickin' his pitchfork in the welds."

"That's a 'triton,' you dumb ox!"

"In Iowa, we call it a pitchfork!"

"The hell with Iowa!"

"You watch yer language in front of the little lady, or I'll stuff both yer ears down yer throat!"

"Sorry, ma'm. Wouldn't offend for the world."

"Got to ask you, Miss Smythe, where did you get those green eyes? They're like to drive me overboard!"

There was no more discussion of data or machinery or danger. The men did not often have the company of a member of the opposite sex, and the words and tone varied between teasing and clear invitation. But there were no unpleasant episodes, and Carol enjoyed both the tour and the attention the growing crowd gave her.

I could be a hundred years old and without teeth, and they would pay me the same due, she thought. And then she reconsidered. *No, they really find me attractive! So did the students on Bygdoy, and Rhys' friends . . I am attractive, and the only man who doesn't see it is Tor Christiansen*!

It was lunch time, and Carol found herself ravenous. The early start and fresh sea air had given her a big appetite. They went back to the flotel dining room.

Tor was already seated at a table with Ole Jenks. He barely glanced up when she and several of her guides joined them. But Ole greeted her with a broad grin and a question about the behavior of her guides.

"They were all perfect gentlemen," she said.

A roar greeted this, and the bantering and jostling continued. Carol felt that Ole encouraged it. *Perhaps he believes that any break in the routine is healthy.*

All through the meal, Carol was aware of the disapproving eyes of Tor on her, judging and admonishing. She tried to ignore him and returned the banter of the men with a determined gaiety, trying to shut him out of her mind by concentrating on the far more pleasant men all around her.

Two contests were being waged simultaneously—one between the men and her, that of innuendo and blatant challenge, and a second between her and Tor, that which had no rules she could understand. She was flattered by the first and annoyed by the second, but the two conflicts within her were disturbingly exciting. It seemed as though she could thrive on conflicts, as though they made her stronger, even exhilarated. The men paying her so much attention were many, Tor only one man.

Tor tolerated the lack of attention accorded him by Ole and the other engineers. He was speaking seriously about stress in the flotel cables, but the men did not seem concerned. Finally, Ole turned to Tor and said, "It's true, the problem grows worse. The computers are showing us signs of disintegration, but we can't tell how much or how fast. I can't see the future, Tor. There are too many variables. All we can do is watch."

"Ole." Tor's voice was strained. "We have to be ready for what might happen."

"Do you have the answers, Tor? How do we 'get ready' for disaster? That's what's really bothering you, isn't it? That we have no answers, no way to be ready."

Tor agreed with a short nod of his head, and the frown lines in his forehead deepened. Carol felt sympathy for him and a sense of guilt for her frivolous enjoyment of this experience. These men took their work seriously. They had to. Any error, mechanical or human, could mean an accident that might cost them their lives. Tor rose abruptly and addressed her in a voice that was meant to carry. "It will be some time before I can leave. Don't get in the way or keep the men from work."

He spoke to her as though she were a child! She felt an angry flush rise to her cheeks, but the jolly voice of Ole broke in before she could respond.

"How could such a slip of a girl get in the way? And the men are much too diligent to be distracted, right?"

The men roared their disagreement and indicated they would prefer to be distracted all day by Carol, but they rose and began to leave the dining room to resume their duties. Alamo directed her to a comfortable reading room, and she set off by herself. She soon found it, deserted, poured herself a cup of coffee from an urn in a corner, and started glancing over the shelves of books and magazines.

An English voice interrupted her solitude. "Excuse me, mum, could I 'ave a word?"

Carol looked up to see a huge, weather-beaten face, darkly handsome, very serious and strangely shy. His shoulders filled the doorway, and his hands nervously twisted the cap he held at his broad chest.

"Of course," said Carol, "please come in. I'm your guest, after all." She smiled as he stepped into the room.

"If I might ask a favor of you . . . you see, my wife lives in London, and she worries terrible about me out here. 'As all kinds of notions about me being tossed about on some tiny raft . . ."

"I can understand that," said Carol, inviting him to sit next to her. "It's natural to worry about someone you care for."

He settled his frame onto the sofa near her, his eyes less evasive. "Yes, mum. Well, I was thinking, it would be a comfort to her if she could talk to you . . . when you go back 'ome, I mean. You being a woman, you could tell her about the rig, 'ow big and safe it is, and all . . ."

"I'd be glad to. I'll ring her up as soon as I get in."

Relief flooded the man's face and he smiled. He was even more handsome when he smiled, and Carol didn't wonder that his wife worried about him, missed him.

"Let me write down her name and number right now."

"I've already done it, mum. It's all right 'ere."

She accepted his neatly printed note. Once she pocketed it, the man relaxed and they began to talk of London, the June weather, neighborhoods they both knew. They discovered they both liked the same little Indian restaurant in Chelsea, and they were laughing about how small the world was when Carol felt someone watching them. She looked up to see Tor standing in the doorway.

He said, "We are leaving, if you are through with your *tete-á-tete.*" As Tor stood there, taut with impatience, Carol smiled brightly at the dark man, deliberately took her time gathering her slicker and handbag, and chatted amenities casually.

The dark man took her hand in both of his. "You will call? You won't lose the number?"

"I promise."

Tor's voice snapped at them like a whip. "An entire crew and boat is waiting for you." He turned on his heel and stomped from the room.

Carol knew she had made her point, however feebly, so she wished her new friend a quick farewell and ran out of the room and down the passageway toward the waiting boat.

It was colder and windier, the sun now hidden behind gray clouds, but their send-off was very warm. The men jostled to come near and shake her hand. Alamo bent over and kissed it to the cheers of the others. They descended into the boat, cast off quickly and headed out into the open sea. As the boat emerged from the shelter of the rig, the wind slapped Carol harshly and an icy spray of salt water splashed into her face. She headed into the boat's cabin.

The captain was at the helm, his mate muttering over a sea chart. She took a seat where she could watch the rig fade into the clouds on the horizon until the boat turned into the wind and headed back toward Stavanger.

Tor entered with a howling blast of wind and slammed the door shut behind him. The men conferred briskly in

Norwegian, pointing and nodding seriously at the dark clouds forming around them. They seemed to come to some agreement, and the captain and mate left the cabin, apparently with Tor's encouragement, leaving the helm to him.

He stood at the wheel, holding it familiarly as his gaze scanned the sea. He was silent, and Carol allowed herself a careful study of him. Her mind began to play with "ifs," dangerous, wishful thoughts—if only he weren't the rudest man she'd ever met, if only he were less angry at the world, if only she could comfort him, were more attractive to him . . .

His words broke into her silent wishes though his eyes never left the sea. "You gave the men much pleasure."

Carol was about to reply that she was glad if she had, but he went on.

"They go for long times without seeing a woman. It was a mistake to take you. Now they will think too much about shore and not concentrate on the work. It is dangerous to forget about the work."

So now she was to be blamed for the behavior of his men. She said nothing but began to burn.

"You should have been more reserved. This was a business trip. I thought you understood that. You behaved like you were on a holiday."

Carol began to breathe deeply, determined to control herself. It had *been* a holiday! Yet she was sure she had learned something of value today. Was work never to be enjoyed? Was life so serious that one could never laugh? She looked at Tor, now silent, apparently finished with his scolding for the moment. She rose and crossed to his side, standing so she could look at his face, so he could see her if he deigned to glance in her direction.

She said, measuring her words so he would not miss either her sense or her determination, "If it was a holiday for me, it was even more so for the men, and I believe they deserved whatever foolishness they allowed themselves. If my presence gave them a chance to have a bit of fun, to be a little less lonely for a few hours, then I'm glad for it." She wanted to go on, but his explosion ripped into her pause.

"You are proud of yourself! Proud that you've teased and flirted with every man on that rig! You've spent the day flinging your curls into the wind, winking your green eyes and making promises. Are you going to keep those promises?"

"You're mad!" She was screaming and didn't care. "You rant and rave like the sea out there, storming against nothing! I've done none of those things! What 'promises'? You can't possibly believe that those big, strong men would be hurt by someone as harmless as I! You overrate my powers, Mr. Christiansen, and you insult my integrity!" She wheeled away from him, but he caught her arm and held it.

"You've a very short memory. You held that man's hand in the reading room, promised to call him, to meet him again. I heard you!"

"No! You have it all wrong! He gave me a London number to call for . . ."

"You think I'm blind? I know what I see. I've seen it before. You're like every other woman . . ."

"Don't be ridiculous. I'm like every other woman? Am I like Solveig? Or Lisle? Like your mother? You're not being fair to me nor to any other woman."

His eyes clouded and he hesitated. "You will not mention my mother in the same breath . . ."

"No? She's different? Of course, she is! She is very special. And how do you treat women who are special to you? You lie to them, you don't tell them you're going out to the rig, out to sea. You deceive them. That's how you treat someone special!"

"That is none of your business! You don't understand . . ."

"You insult her! You don't even know her. She's the strongest woman I've ever met. What if something should happen? What if there were an accident and you were hurt? She would suffer your agony, and she would have to bear the insult of your not trusting her. She deserves your trust, and so, for that matter, do I!"

His words came out slowly, painfully, as he fought for control. "Mor has suffered much. I protect her. It would do no good for her to worry." A shudder rippled across his shoulders, and a sound, soft and deep within him, emerged from him like from a giant child, helpless in its pain. He put his head down on the wheel and was quiet.

Carol didn't move, didn't breathe. She knew his agony had passed. He had been flung out of the maelstrom and found a calmer sea for the moment.

The captain and mate returned, laughing and carrying a thermos of coffee and extra cups. Without a word, Tor turned the wheel over to the mate and left the cabin. The mate grabbed the wheel, which started to spin, and the captain looked at Carol questioningly. She managed a smile and took the thermos and cups from him, and turned away. She heard him grunt and walk away toward the mate.

She managed to pour a cup of coffee in spite of her trembling hands. She sat and held it tightly, allowing the warmth to penetrate them, willing them to stop shaking. After a few minutes, she stood up and looked out the forward windows of the cabin.

Tor stood on deck at the prow, the waves dashing his still form, the wind tearing at his hair. He was like a fig-urehead, strong and wooden against the sea, rigid and unyielding—against the sea, himself, and the rest of his world. She tried to keep her heart from going out to him, tried to think about the argument. Had she won it, or at least made a point? But she knew, staring at the lonely man out there in the wind, that no one had won anything.

Chapter Ten

IT WAS MANY hours before they were alone together, in Tor's car as they drove from the Bergen heliport to the house. He hadn't spoken to her nor she to him.

The silence between them had wearied Carol more than the difficult, strenuous trip. The boat had taken longer to reach Stavanger because of the increasingly rough weather. The jeep had become mired in the muddy road in the town. And there had been a delay while Tor and the helicopter pilot argued about the risk of a flight back to Bergen. They had finally agreed they were enough ahead of the storm and took off for a very rough flight. If it hadn't been for the silence, the tense, tiring silence, Carol might have been able to think of the journey as another adventure, an episode to be remembered and chatted about in some mythical future conversation. But she had not noticed very much, nor even worried about the storm, the sea, or the flight. *It's out of my hands, all of it,* she had kept repeating to herself.

The drive back to the house continued under the oppressive silence. She didn't care. She was tired and hungry. She thought, *I want food and a bed, and I want to get away from Tor . . . only a few more minutes.*

At last they drove up to the house and started toward the door. Just as Tor reached out to open it, it was flung open. Solveig Folkdahl stood there, her perfection marred by the fury in her face.

"Where have you been?!" Her voice was a scream.

Carol felt the body beside her pause and slump, a sigh coming long and low from it, the body that had to be as tired as her own. He had come from one battle only to face another. But Carol couldn't allow his battles to be hers, not anymore. She brushed past Solveig in the doorway and escaped to the kitchen, thinking *Let them go at it; they deserve each other. I'm going to get something to eat.*

The kitchen backed onto the study, and she could hear everything. Solveig's voice pierced the wall very clearly, and even Tor's mumbled replies were audible. They spoke in English, their language of choice, apparently, for arguments. Carol hurried to fix herself something to eat, trying to shut out the voices, but their edges cut through the walls into her, despite her efforts.

"You will not treat me like some convenience! Like someone you keep in reserve for your public appearances! You'll not run off with some little tramp without a word to me!"

"She is not a tramp. We were working."

"Working? And you work so hard you don't see the green eyes studying you, appraising, thinking like the cat about to strike its prey? You cannot be that dull, Tor!"

"Solveig, I'm very tired. And you've no right to ..."

"I've every right! I've waited four years, and before that, all my life. It has always been understood ..."

"*You* have possibly understood something. I never ..."

"Tor, don't try to avoid this, to avoid me. You know perfectly well that I ... that we've always known ..."

"Solveig, stop! You feel very sorry for yourself, don't you? Poor little princess, waiting in your tower? Not for me, Solveig. You've never waited for me. The truth is that you love your tower, your perfect world. You don't want to leave it for anyone."

"That's ridiculous! You're trying to avoid the responsibility. I'm a living, breathing woman, Tor. I have feelings."

"I didn't say that you didn't, but ..."

"People *expect* it, Tor!" Solveig's voice became more strident, louder. "I will not be the woman that Tor Christ iansen turned away from *twice*! First for your American tramp, now for this English ..."

"You will not speak of Joleen!" Tor's voice rose in fury.

"Face it, Tor, she was a tramp, and you know it. She slept with every man she met, and many she had never met. Even Rhys ..."

"You will be silent!"

Tor's voice was awful in its anger, but Solveig continued, her every word coldly cutting, unafraid, unthreatened.

"She fooled you, played with you, dishonored you at every opportunity. And you ... you treated her like a delicate flower, thinking you protected her. You acted as though you were some kind of warrior and she a virginal princess. But she was a whore, and you a fool."

There was silence. Carol held her breath, afraid to move. She knew she shouldn't be listening, that it was none of her business. But she could not move from the center of the kitchen, not even reach out to grasp a chair.

Tor's voice was low, vibrating with tension. "You don't know what you're talking about."

"I know no more than everyone else in Norway, I admit that! But enough of your tramps. I want to talk about us, about the plans, what you owe to me for these years of ..."

"I owe you nothing."

"You owe me everything!"

"You speak of the money? The business? You have made good your investment many times over."

"I speak of my investment in you, Tor."

"I was never part of any arrangement, any deal. I have never put myself up for sale."

"I've earned you!"

Tor's voice rose again. "I'm not an object to acquire! You try to own me. You want me to decorate the empty space at your side—in the right clothes, the right style. You can find someone else to fill the void, Solveig. You can have any man you want, as long as he's weak enough!"

There was a long pause. Finally Solveig spoke, her voice icy clear. "How like a man, to ignore the facts, to avoid the issue. You refuse to commit to me, to the future, to anything. I don't need anyone to fill my 'void,' as you call it. I will deal with you no longer. I am walking away from you! Understand that! *I* am the one who is walking away."

There was silence after that until the front door opened and slammed shut, soon followed by the engine of Solveig's car screaming to life and then fading into the distance. In another moment, the door opened and closed again. Carol found some strength left in her legs and walked to a window. She saw Tor walking across the meadow, head down, striding against the wind toward the sea. She watched until he disappeared behind the cliffs.

She stared down at the sandwich she had prepared, not remembering when she had done it. She couldn't touch it. What she really needed was a drink, a strong one. She went into the sitting room to pour herself a brandy, then sat sipping it slowly in front of the fireplace. The glow that was so cheerful before now seemed sputtering, struggling to stay alive.

Tomorrow she would be gone and all that had happened in only ten days would be memory. The memories of the towering mountains and gentle valleys would dim, the color of the fjords and sky and Tor's eyes would fade. All the intensity of those visions would evaporate in London's gray light, and she would be able to rest. She would resume her steady, tame life.

But even as she assured herself of that future, sipping the golden liquid that eased and burned, she knew none of it would fade for a very long time, perhaps never. And she knew that she felt something intense and real for Tor Christiansen, the man who turned away from a beautiful, rich woman in favor of a mistaken memory.

She felt his presence before she saw him. She looked up to see him standing in the doorway. His hair was damp lying flat against his head, and she thought, *It must have begun to rain.* How such inconsequential things could intrude so suddenly on strong feelings! *I'm dying to run to him, and I think about the weather!* she thought.

He moved to the fire and placed a fresh log on it. He did not speak, nor did she, for a long time. He looked so tired. The flickering light from the fire, hungrily licking the dry wood, lit his brow and shadowed the tiny lines at the corners of his mouth. She knew she should leave him alone, but she could not move. She wanted so much to hold him, to touch and soothe the troubled face. At last she put down her glass and started to get up, to go away and leave him in peace.

"Do not go. Please." His voice was low, undemanding.

Carol settled back on the sofa and waited quietly.

"You heard?"

"Yes. I'm sorry . . . I was in the kitchen, and . . ."

"It doesn't matter. It is over now."

"I'm sorry, Tor."

"No, it is good that it is over . . . good for both of us. Solveig must have a life, and she cannot have it with me."

"And your life, Tor; what of your life?"

He took his eyes from the fire and looked at her. The light behind him shadowed his face, and she couldn't read anything that might be there. She had spoken too personally.

He said, "You were caught in my life, Carol, for this short time. I'm sorry for it, for all of it. You must escape it, as quickly as you can."

She couldn't answer. She knew he was right, speaking now so calmly, so reasonably. She must leave here, leave him, or she would be torn to pieces by the swirling currents of his life and her own heart. But she was drawn to him like the fingers of the fjords reaching deep into the land, like the land reaching out into the sea.

"Tor, if I've caused any of this, I want you to know that I never intended for anyone to be hurt—least of all you."

159

He sighed and moved to the sofa beside her and gently took her hand in his. "You have done nothing to hurt, Carol. Me, I've not been hurt. I've not felt hurt for many years. Only anger, yes ... and pride. And now I feel nothing at all. And I am glad I feel nothing. You must not pity me. You must take the softness from your eyes, for your sake."

He was so near, so warm, so very sad. Her hand went to touch his cheek, and she did not prevent it. "Nothing, Tor? You feel nothing?"

He did not reject her hand on his face, nor did he seem to feel it. She let her fingers trace the line of his brow, the skin warm from the fire.

"Rhys calls me a robot, when he has the courage or interest to face me ... an automaton. I think he is right."

She withdrew her exploring hand from his face. He did not seem to notice. She folded her hands in her lap, holding them tightly together.

"You must have loved her very much—the American girl."

The short laugh was almost brutal, surprising her. "I did. I loved her with every part of me, completely, extravagantly. And I was the fool Solveig called me just now, what others have called me for years. At first, I didn't know about Joleen, about the other men. I only knew that I wanted her. But soon I knew the truth, and it was too late. I would not admit it, to myself or anyone else. I told myself that I could contain her, tame her to my will. I continued to believe that I could have done it if she hadn't died. But I was wrong to think that, to dream that. I didn't have that power when she was alive, and I do not have any such power now. I constructed a fantasy so complete, so solid, that it withstood the assault of logic. Can you understand how hard it's been, even with all my great engineering skills, to demolish a fantasy?"

"Tor, I know what it is not to feel—to try not to feel. Not

feeling, not speaking out, protected me for years. I was a mouse in my safe, gray corner. Not feeling is safe. But you, Tor, you must . . ."

"I don't want . . ."

"You must forgive yourself for your fantasy, and for your pride. All you have to do is admit you're human, and then you can absolve yourself."

He was silent, and Carol could say no more. She sat there, the helpless feeling welling up inside her like the tears she would not allow to pour from her eyes. There were no more arguments, no logic in her head. It was not reason that made her lift her hands and turn his face to hers. It was not sense that made her gently place her mouth on his. There were no words to say, and she reached out to him physically.

His lips were firm and warm against hers. She felt his hands cover her own, and he took them gently from his face and kissed the palms softly.

"Thank you, Carol." It was a real "thank you," an acknowledgment of her expression of concern. He went on, his voice soft. "You are so lovely, both strong and soft. And I thank you for this moment."

Carol laughed quietly, ruefully. "I'm not at all strong, I'm afraid. I seem to have done one stupid thing after another, every since I stepped off the airplane in Oslo."

"No, that's not true. Don't think that. You are very strong, stronger than even the 'Sardine Queen,' I think."

Carol looked at him with surprise. "You know about that? Lisle said that she and Rhys named her that."

"I heard them laugh about it. They named her correctly. Rhys and Lisle are quick to find the truth and put it into a healthy perspective, to burst balloons of pretense. There was a time I shared in that, when the three of us could see the truth, the joke in many things. When I heard them laugh about the 'Sardine Queen,' I thought of 'Herring Heiress.' It is funny in English, isn't it?" Carol laughed and nodded, her laughter so close to tears she had to look away. "I wanted to join them, to tell them my little joke, but I could not ... not before I lost it to my anger, or to the wind."

"You'll find it again, Tor. You must. We all have to laugh sometimes, to keep from crying."

The tears welling up in her eyes spilled over. He frowned and kissed them away. "You must laugh only. You must not cry for Tor Christiansen, the man of ice and snow."

The heat from his body belied his words as he drew her to him, cradling her in one strong arm, touching her face with his hand. It all felt so warm, so easy, so right. His hand moved through her hair, around her shoulders.

She rubbed her cheek against his hard, warm chest, her own hand moving to learn him, touching the broadness of his shoulders, finding the muscular strength in his arms, moving around the open collar of his shirt where the soft curls spiraled and waved between her fingers. The pulse in his throat was beating strongly. And she could feel her own heart, fast and light against that heavy, steady throb. His hair was still faintly damp from the rain, the tendrils at the back of his muscular neck still warm and wet.

It was as though they were living warmly in some other stratum—a place where everything was slower, every sensation heightened. There was no sense of time. Everything had stopped and was waiting for them to explore one another. His hands were calloused but light, tentative on her face. His fingers searched her hair and found and caressed her ears, then moved to her forehead and eyelids, stroking them so gently they quieted under the touch. She felt the tiny sensation as his finger played with her lashes, and though her eyes were hungry for the sight of him, she could not open them. Then his hand moved down her cheeks, circling to her mouth. Her lips parted, and she felt the rush of warm wetness on them as his hand moved around her neck and his mouth came to hers and parted, his tongue reaching, searching, hungry.

Carol wanted desperately to let the precious time, the precious moment, go on forever. She wanted to keep the thought from coming into her mind. She didn't want to think, didn't want her mind to prevent what her body wanted. But the tiny voice began to grow, words and memory, a voice she could not ignore. *He said he had no feeling for any woman, no feelings at all. This isn't something special for him. It's only a need to hold someone for a moment, a moment that won't ever be repeated.* The counter-argument formed in her mind immediately. *It doesn't matter! There's only now, so let it go on!* She couldn't believe that the man who held her, whom she could feel so alive in her arms, did not feel something— something that overwhelmed him as much as her.

But the voice would not relent; the conflict throbbed and grew until the tears streamed from her, and a sob wrenched from her throat.

Tor's body's stiffened, pausing in the passionate quest when he heard the cry. He lifted his head away from hers and looked into her eyes through the tears. His fingers touched the wetness wonderingly, concerned.

He thinks that it's something he's done, she thought, and she reached out to reassure him.

But he pulled back from her. The contact was lost, the pulsing current between them gone. The space between them was small, but it may as well have been a mile. Tor turned away, his arms clasped in front of him. Carol sat up and pulled her knees close to her breast, hugging them tightly. She felt so small, so alone, as though a part of her being was gone, forever lost.

They sat in silence for a time, breathing their bodies back into control and their minds back to rationality.

Tor's voice broke a little when he finally spoke. "We are both very tired. We are too vulnerable now—to each other, to everything. I don't ever want to hurt you, to see you hurt."

She didn't want to say anything; she wanted to reach out and touch him, draw him back into her arms. If she could only find some way to let him know everything she felt, everything she thought. But she could only manage, in a small voice, to respond to his words. "I'm not hurt, Tor, not at all. I'm confused and ... of course, you're right. We're both very tired. I wish ..."

His bitter laugh cut into her words. He said, "No, of course you are not hurt. You are stronger than I. I am so blind. When I first saw you, first heard your voice, I wanted to protect you. I should find a weak woman, one who will make me feel that I am strong, that I am needed to protect her."

Carol wanted more than anything to tell him how much she needed him at that moment and forever, but he went on.

"But I do not care for weak women, nor even those who pretend to be weak. I admire, am attracted to the strong, the women who want and struggle and fight, who are not afraid to show they are strong. You are such a woman, and yet now you seem so soft, so giving and gentle. That is more frightening."

"Frightening? But Tor ..."

"I must not be afraid, Carol. I must not even speak of it anymore."

Carol felt helpless before his words, his strange and conflicting rationale. "I don't understand, Tor. Why be afraid of gentleness, or of strength, in someone else? Or in yourself? There isn't a weak bone in your body. How can you be afraid ... ?"

The telephone rang in the hall outside the living room. It was a gentle, distant sound, but it jarred them both to silence. Neither of them moved, neither spoke. Someone picked up the phone, but the greater silence, the one between Carol and Tor, continued. Carol waited, wanting to draw more from Tor, but he said nothing. Tiny beads of sweat stood out on his brow, and the muscles in his neck were taut, straining.

There was a sharp rap on the door to the room, and Helge's voice called through it urgently. "Tor!" It is your office. There is trouble."

Tor rose quickly, his body springing as though it had been coiled under some rigid vise. The action released him, and he almost ran out of the room. She heard him speak briefly and quietly to Helge in the hall, then move away toward the phone.

Carol could not move. She grasped her knees harder against herself, holding on with every ounce of strength she had. Finally her arms cramped and she released them, but she did not let go of her feelings. Perhaps there were none left.

Helge came into the room and crossed to the fire. She looked at Carol curiously, glancing at her as she poked the fire to more life. Carol hoped her face held nothing but a question about the phone call.

"It is the storm. The flotel, you know . . . there is too much list. They are worried."

For the first time Carol became conscious of the wind. It howled above the roof and threw its weight against the windows. A driving rain had begun and was pelting the glass in bursts of wind and wet fury.

Tor appeared in the doorway dressed in his yellow slicker. He pulled a heavy woolen hat over his hair and flipped the hood of the slicker over it. "I must go to the office. I must be there when the computer data comes in. The weld on one of the sea legs may snap . . . it could be very bad. Please, go to bed and do not worry. There is nothing you can do."

Then he left, the wind howling through the open doorway before he pulled it shut behind him. A cold draft swept through the hall and across the room, spreading its chill over Carol on the sofa.

"You would like some coffee?" Helge's voice was soft, almost shy. Carol looked up into her gentle eyes.

She knows, thought Carol. *She sees it in my face, and perhaps she saw it in Tor's. And she feels for both of us.* "No, thank you. I'm afraid it will keep me awake. I really am tired and must get some sleep tonight."

"Of course. But you will not mind if I make some for myself? I won't sleep tonight, not until Tor returns."

"But he told you there was nothing . . ."

"It doesn't matter. It is foolish, I know, but I am still a mother. And mothers wait for their sons to come home, no matter how late the hour, or how old they grow."

Helge set up a little grate over the glowing fire in the fireplace. From a cabinet she pulled a big, scarred coffee pot and filled it with water from the bar. She dumped a heaping cup of coffee directly into the water and put the pot over the fire. There was a feeling of ritual in her movements, in her concentration on the simple task.

"It's the way I used to make it, waiting for Chris to come from the boat, when I was home with the babies. Boiled coffee, it is the best. When it is done I break an egg into it, to settle the grounds."

She sat on the sofa with Carol, and they both stared into the fire. Both minds were on Tor, out there in the storm. And then Carol thought of the rig and the giant, laughing men aboard her. She grew restless, thinking of the waves lashing the structure, the rain driving along the decks, the wind howling in the open sea. She thought of the Englishman and Alamo and Ole Jenks.

Terms floated through her tired mind—incoherent jumbles of scrawls and words. *Flotel—semi-submersible—anchored to the sea bottom on five sea legs—giant cables—welded joints that allowed some flexibility in the legs—knees of the cables—sea cur-*

166

rents ... *welds* ... something about the welds! It was in the last file! Carol jumped to her feet and ran to Tor's study.

Helge, startled, followed her. "Carol, what's wrong?"

"It's in the last file. I finished typing it late last night. Tor hasn't read it yet. He probably hasn't even noticed that it's finished. He knew it was a scrawled muddle . . . hadn't worked on it himself at all . . ."

Carol paged rapidly through the file until she came to the section headed "Weld Strength" and read down to "On-site procedures, subsection three . . ." She read no further but ran to the telephone.

"I don't know if this new data will help, but Tor should know about it."

The phone rang endlessly, emptily in Tor's office. Helge stood by, patient but very anxious.

"No one answers in his office. He must be in another part of the building . . . the computer room!"

Carol dialed again, another number, then a third. She listened to the ringing at the other end of the line, frustrated. She looked at Helge, at the deep concern in the mother's face. She hung up the phone and took Helge's hands.

"I'm sure everything will be all right. I can't imagine anything happening to the flotel. It's so enormous, like an island. It feels as solid as dry land. No mere storm could possibly . . ."

Helge's hands gripped hers suddenly, harshly. Her eyes were alert, questioning. "How do you know this? About the flotel?"

Carol's breath caught in her throat. She had meant to comfort the woman, not to betray anything. Helge's eyes were penetrating and held her own, held her to the truth. "I was there. Today. Tor took me to the rig."

When Carol saw the look that washed over the woman's face, she wished she had lied, wished she had spared the woman the knowledge of her son's deception.

"Tor went to the rig?"

"Yes, he wanted to spare you . . . said you would worry . . ."

"Carol, you must tell me! He goes there often?"

"He said he has to keep close watch over the whole operation. But I'm sure it's perfectly safe, Helge. He wouldn't . . ."

Helge grasped Carol's arm. "Carol, he goes there now!"

Carol protested, "But he couldn't, not in this weather. He'd have to take the helicopter, and the storm makes that far too dangerous . . ."

"I tell you, he goes now!"

Without another word, Helge rushed to a closet and tore two coats from it. She threw one to Carol and wrapped herself in the other.

"What is going on?" Lisle's sleepy voice questioned them from the top of the stairs.

Her mother barked sharply and Lisle's eyes widened to full wakefulness. "The coffee pot is on the fire in the living room! Let it boil for a few more minutes, take it off, break an egg into it. Keep it warm for us!"

Carol was in awe of the woman as the two of them braced themselves and ran out into the storm to the car. She had dealt with Lisle and gotten the two of them out of the house in a matter of seconds. But surely she was wrong about Tor! Surely he wouldn't try to take off in this storm!

Helge threw her the car keys. "My eyes are not good at night. Drive to the heliport as fast as you can without killing us."

Carol didn't hesitate. Mistaken or not, the woman was in command. Carol started the car and accelerated smoothly. She drove faster than she would have liked with the rain pelting down on the windscreen, the gusts sometimes washing over it completely and obliterating the view. The wind seemed to almost lift the car off the street. She remembered the route Tor had driven that morning, and

Helge corrected her whenever she hesitated. They were at the heliport in ten long minutes.

"Drive out onto the pad!" Helge's eyes and pointing hand indicated a brightly lighted area. Carol could see the whirring blades of the aircraft already in motion. Men were running, moving through the light and the rain. Carol pulled the car as close as she dared and turned off the engine. She and Helge bolted out of either side of the car and were greeted by angry shouts from all sides, telling them to move the car back, to get out of the way.

Helge ignored them all and went straight for the helicopter. One man tried to stop her until he saw who she was, then backed off and pointed to a group of men near the vehicle. Carol followed Helge, the rain slashing at her face, the wind and sound amplified by the blades so near them.

Tor saw them. He stepped apart from the group of men. His face registered shock when he saw his mother charging toward him. When he saw Carol, he scowled.

Carol thought, *He thinks I've betrayed him. And perhaps I have. I haven't time to worry about it now!* She rushed past Helge and pulled the file from under her coat.

Shouting to be heard over the noise of storm and engine, she thrust the file into his hands. "Pages ten through fourteen! Weld joints! Read it!"

Her words registered. Tor took the file and moved to the shelter of an overhang on the hangar. He opened the file and began to read by the light of the glaring flood-lamps. Maybe it didn't mean anything. Maybe it had nothing to do with the problem, maybe . . . But Tor had found something to cause him to read closely and turn the pages with speed and care. Carol and Helge huddled near him, quiet. Carol noticed, irrelevantly, that her neatly typed pages were curling and smearing in the rain. Tor closed the file with a decisive motion and looked toward the helicopter.

Helge's voice carried clearly as she grasped Tor's arm.

"You will call to the rig. They can fix it there. You do not fly in this storm and kill yourself!"

Tor barely glanced at her. He moved away and shouted to a man nearby, whom Carol recognized as the pilot who had flown them to Stavanger that morning. The pilot nodded, pulled his cap lower over his ears, and headed for the aircraft. Tor pushed the file under his slicker and started after him.

Helge shouted, "Tor! You will not do this!"

Tor turned back to her. "This is no time to argue! We have two hundred men on that rig. I might have been able to help before, but with this information, I can try a new way to stabilize the platform. I'm wasting time, Mor!"

"If you go, you will not come home! You will not come to my house! You are no longer my son!" The fear and pain in Helge's voice belied her anger.

Carol knew she had no right to interfere, no right to touch either mother or son. But she could not stop herself. She grabbed Helge by her shoulders and turned her around, away from Tor. "Helge! He must do what he feels is right! Give him your love and trust! Give that to him now! Don't let him go with anger!"

Helge stared at her. "He must not go. The sea will take him. I know it as I knew the night it took his father."

There was terrible fear in her eyes, and Carol turned to see the same fear in Tor's. But he turned away toward the helicopter.

Carol grabbed his arm and screamed above the horrible noise, above the fear. "Tor! Call first! At least, call first! Radio to Ole, give him instructions. Trust your men! You'll be in the air for hours. You could be too late. Call, Tor! A few hours may make all the difference!"

She felt the tension and the strength in him, the sense of what she said penetrating his stubbornness, the rush of his brave impulse. He took his eyes from her and signaled to the pilot, who was about to motion him aboard. The engine geared down, and the noise level lowered.

"Tor, it is your decision. You're too responsible to risk your life when reason says it might be foolish. But it's your decision, Tor. And only yours."

She could not read his expression. Everything was moving too fast. Abruptly he turned from her and shouted orders to the men. Then he ran inside the hangar. Through a window they could see him push the radio operator from his chair in front of the console, barking orders.

Carol wanted to run in after him, to stay with him, to be with him—even to fly out over the sea that threatened and challenged him. But she could not bring herself to go inside the hangar. *I've gone too far as it is,* she thought. *I don't dare intrude any further.*

She turned toward Helge with dread. She had to face the worst, to know what her outburst, her direct countermand of Mor's demands to her son, had done. But Helge was already walking to the car, head down, totally alone in the driving rain. Carol ran after her.

The ride home was wordless. Carol felt the tension in the silent woman beside her, but her heart and thoughts were with the man in the storm. She knew she would never see him again. Whatever happened, she would be on her way to London before he returned. The bleak, relentless storm whirled around her, but the cold dark void inside her, growing bigger and emptier, was more frightening. The whole idea of "home" seemed pale and unattractive. There was no instinct, no magnetic pull toward her native country. Instead, she felt as though she were being flung away to England, away from this angry land, this sea, away from Tor's arms.

Lights burned in every window of the house. Rhys and Lisle waited for them at the door, with Inga and Grete hovering closely behind them. Their mood was somber but practical, helping them out of wet clothes, forcing steaming mugs of hot milk and brandy into their cold hands. Helge allowed herself to be helped and warmed, but she was quiet. It fell to Carol to explain the situation as well as she could.

Rhys pulled a heavy sweater over his head and grabbed a slicker. "I'm going out to the heliport. I can't sit here all night and wonder what's going on."

Helge broke from her passive state and reached out to him. "There isn't anything you can do, Rhys. What will be, will be. Stay here."

"I know I can't do anything, but I want to be there. At least I can be that close to him. I must." He held his mother close for a moment. "I'll be back. We'll both be back." He grinned at her, kissed the tip of her nose and went out into the storm.

Carol felt an impulse to run after Rhys, to see Tor one more time. But the warm drink clouded her senses and every muscle in her body felt sapped of any strength. She let Inga almost carry her up the stairs to her room. And she was aware of Grete and Lisle, gently leading, and cajoling Helge into hers. All the words were gentle, cheerful non-sense. These women, they knew what to do at times like these.

Inga undressed her and tucked her into the feather bed as though she were a child. She felt very much like one, helpless and weak, her body exhausted, her mind a sea of confusion, her spirit dull. She wanted to stay awake, to think, to know the worst. But there was no escape from sleep nor the dreams that came to her.

At first there were no wild images—merely events re-curring and repeating. The storm she had just been in, her own words and those of Helge and Tor over the roar of the helicopter. She fell deeper into her sleep, deeper into her dream. A sea swirling madly before her. Above it, the rig, far in the distance and yet close, receding and drawing near until it was almost on top of her. Then it drew back, raised majestically in the gray clouds, strong and sure,

172

steady in the midst of the violent gray water. And then it was no longer the mechanical island, but a man . . . a man standing tall in the prow of a Viking ship, his body taut and strong against the wind. The image blurred and began to tip into the gray waves, the once upright figure slowly listing to one side, with no struggle, no resistance—just a gentle, inevitable fall into the sea. Carol reached out to it, reaching out to keep it upright, to keep it above the gray horizon, to hold it, to keep it . . .

The straining, forward movement of her sleeping body woke her. She was damp from perspiration, breathing hard, twisted in the comforter on the bed. She opened her eyes to a gray dawn. The storm was over.

She rose and showered quickly. While she dressed, she could hear voices below. Perhaps there was some news. She glanced at her suitcase but put the departure that it symbolized out of her mind and ran down the stairs.

The smell of hot coffee greeted her just before Inga appeared from the kitchen, Grete behind her laden with a heavy tray filled with steaming mugs, fresh breads, mountains of scrambled eggs laced with smoked salmon.

"Come," said Inga, "you need something in your stomach!" She added, more quietly, "There is no news."

Carol followed the procession into the living room where Helge and Lisle waited. Lisle leapt up to greet her and then fussed with Inga and Grete over the breakfast, but their chatter faded into the background as Helge rose and approached Carol. Carol turned to the woman she had defied the night before, afraid she had lost her friendship. But Helge stood before her with warmth and concern in her eyes, and she reached her arms out to Carol. Helge cared for the way she felt! And Carol threw her arms around the older woman. The embrace she felt returned was strong and comforting. Carol knew that Helge did not demonstrate affection often or capriciously. The embrace was rare and meaningful.

173

Helge released her and took her hand. She felt the other taken by Lisle, and they led her to the sofa. Carol realized that she was crying, her eyes blinded by tears she had held back for so many hours of waking and sleeping agony. She sat down and was handed a handkerchief.

Inga and Grete fussed over the trays, performing noisily, breaking the tension in the room, distracting all of them from torment with lively argument over the mundane. They poured and buttered, sliced and arranged. They forced food onto her and Helge and Lisle. Lisle wolfed hers down, but Helge and Carol could only pick and sip, however much this dismayed their cooks. They pouted and pretended to take it all very personally, affronted that their breakfast was not devoured. But they knew very well it was not the food; the food was there to fill the waiting time rather than stomachs. There was love in the gesture, and Carol felt grateful to be a recipient.

They all heard the car driving up outside at the same moment, and the chatter stopped immediately. The five women ran out into the hall. The door opened and Rhys burst in.

"The conquering heroes return, ya? Where is breakfast?" He hugged his mother and lifted Lisle high in the air. There were more words in Norwegian, but the sense was triumph.

Carol smiled at Rhys but hurried past him to the doorway. And Tor was there, his eyes tired, his shoulders slumped. He looked up at her and spoke. "We are all right Ole was able to line the weak cable to a strut and weld it tight. The storm eased, and the flotel straightened enough so we can go in and repair it now. We were very lucky. And thanks to you, we could take advantage of our luck. The file you remembered gave us the key." He hesitated, looking at her in a new way. If Carol hadn't known better, she

174

might have called that new way "shy," but she knew it couldn't be.

"I'm glad, Tor . . ." she began.

But Helge's joyful greeting to Tor interrupted her. Tor turned to his mother and embraced her. "Mor, I am sorry. But you see, I have come back to you. I die a little when I hurt you."

"Where is the coffee?!" Rhys demanded. "I shall die if I do not have coffee!" And the Christiansens laughed and gathered about the trays, a sudden healthy hunger replacing the tension and emotions of the moment. Inga and Grete scurried to supplement what was already enough for an army.

Carol stood apart in the doorway watching the laughing family, hugging and teasing each other. This was no place, no time for a stranger. She slipped quietly away and went outside, eager to be alone. She wanted to taste one last time the sea-mountain air, to breathe the color of the wild flowers, to touch the hills. The sky was beginning to clear; her flight would leave on time.

She walked into the meadow, her hands deep inside the pockets of her skirt against the chill of the cold-washed air. The ground was damp beneath her feet, the grasses just beginning to unbend from the lashing of the storm, just beginning to seek the midsummer sunlight that broke through the high clouds. She climbed a huge, lonely boulder and sat staring out towards the sound of the sea. The morning breeze tingled lightly on her arms. She felt naked, cool, the clean damp air penetrating the thin cloth of her blouse. She would remember this moment forever and forget all the rest. She would wash the hurt and confusion from her mind and remember this place, this little place only.

She did not hear him approaching her in the soft grass, but suddenly she knew he was there. He came around the boulder and looked at her as she perched, tiny and alone, at the level of his broad chest. He carried a thick wool lap robe over one arm.

"Mor worries you will be cold," Tor said. "She sends this to put around you if you wish."

Carol opened her mouth to thank him, but no words came. He had stopped her tongue with his presence. He was so tall and strong against the morning sun. His thick hair, disheveled from the night's storm, curled around his ears. His rough shirt was open at the throat, and a glistening of sweat on his skin shone beneath the damp curls. His chest expanded and contracted under the shirt. He was breathing hard. He had been running! Still he did not move.

"You are truly the little sea maiden, perched on your rock, waiting for the fish to come and play. But there will be no fish today, there is only me." With that Tor reached out and lifted her off the rock and drew her into his arms, engulfing her in his embrace. She shivered to feel the heat of his body on her cool skin.

He carried her to the side of the boulder where the sun had almost dried the grass. Holding her with one arm, he threw the robe to the ground, then lowered her gently down to it, spreading it out to protect her from the dampness. But she wouldn't have cared about wet grass. The warmth of his body close to hers spread heat like a blanket. His sweet salty mouth kissed her hungrily, tasting and drinking of her. She licked the salt from his lips, her mouth as hungry as his.

The sun scattered the clouds above them, clearing its domain into vivid blueness. Tor raised his head over hers, and his eyes were the same blue, the same clear blue. "You are uncomfortable?" he said softly.

"No," she whispered sadly, feeling as though the word would stop the world rushing around her. But there must be words. The moment had to end. She would miss her plane, and she didn't know which would be the greater torture—to have one more hour or one more day.

His arms engulfed her, holding her close to him. She laid her head under his chin and he kissed her hair. "It is good that I can keep you warm. The summer is very short, you know. And the winter nights are long and cold. To stay warm, two people must stay very close, all the winter nights."

Carol moved her head back to look up into his face, her green eyes puzzled. "The winter?"

He nestled her against him. "Very cold, and very dark, and very long. It is necessary to 'bundle' for long times, and only get out of the warm bed for coffee and *hadstu*."

"Tor, my flight is . . . my job . . . Mr. McKinzie is . . ."

"We will name our first son after him. McKinzie Christ-iansen! Is good, ya? And we will give him to Mor to play with while we hold each other in our warm feather bed."

Carol sat up slowly over him, and then put her hands on the strong face. It was time for words now. "Tor, are you sure? You want me to stay? After all the . . ."

He put his finger to her lips. His words came slowly, softly. "I want you to stay forever. I love you, Carol."

She heard the words, but every fiber of her common sense told her to push them from her mind.

"Carol, I know what you must think of me. I know I hurt you, but I will never hurt you again. I swear it. My hurting you was my fighting against myself, against feeling love for you. I was afraid from the first moment I saw you. And from the time in our meadow, I grew more afraid. I wanted you to disappear, and I wanted to protect you. Your strength angered me, and your gentleness frightened me. But last night, you gave me your strength and your understanding. You freed me from Mor's demands and my own insane impulse to fly to the rig. You gave me my choice, and that made me strong. You freed me from many other things. And I need you to keep me free. I need your strength to remind me of mine, your gentleness to awake my own."

A thousand objections flashed through her mind, but he touched the frown on her forehead, smoothing it with his warm hand, and she was quiet.

"You asked me once what it was like to be on the ski jump, and I could not answer you. But I know the words now, because my life has been like that feeling for many years. The jumper pushes off from the top, filled with tensions, crouched and ready to spring at the tip of the jump. But in my life for so long there has been no tip, no end of the slope. I have been riding down an endless slide, coiled and rigid, never seeing, never reaching the take-off. And now, with you, I have found it. We have begun to soar through the air, high and free. You must not worry. We are going to have a perfect landing."

He kissed her tenderly, with a tormenting delicacy that made the sun whirl in the midsummer sky above them.

"Carol, say you will stay, please."

Carol gasped for breath, but her voice was sure, as sure as her mind. "Ya, I will stay, Tor Christiansen . . . for the perfect landing and many more rides!"

Tor rose and pulled her up to stand beside him. He picked up the robe and draped it around her shoulders, then took her hand and kissed it. He smiled at her, and the joyful light in his eyes was reflected in her own. With hands joined, they turned and ran together, toward the house, toward home.